Callum's

Hope

A Curvy Girl Age-Gap Romance

Nichole Rose

Cover Photographer: Jenn Leblanc

Cover Artist: Yoly at Cormar Covers

CONTENTS

About the Book   1

Chapter One   3

Chapter Two   9

Chapter Three   16

Chapter Four   26

Chapter Five   36

Chapter Six   45

Chapter Seven   56

Chapter Eight   66

Chapter Nine   77

Chapter Ten   91

Chapter Eleven   102

Chapter Twelve   112

Chapter Thirteen   121

Epilogue   127

Author's Note   132

Silver Spoon Falls   133

Dear Mr. Dad Bod   135

Instalove Book Club   138

Nichole's Book Beauties   139

Follow Nichole   140

More By Nichole Rose   142

About Nichole Rose   147

ABOUT THE BOOK

Finding love on St. Patrick's Day was not part of this bodyguard's assignment...

Callum

I've heard enough about the water in Silver Spoon Falls to know two things:

The people here don't joke about it. And I need to stay away from it.

But the luck of the Irish clearly isn't on my side.

Because I just got hired to protect the woman who bottles and sells it.

One look at Hope Byrne has me rethinking everything.

Starting with how soon I can make her mine.

There's something magical about this curvy little goddess and her fiery Irish spirit.

And I fully intend to break all my rules to claim her.

Hope

Thanks to the water, people in this town have always been lucky in love.

Why shouldn't others benefit too?

Giving them a little bit of hope makes me happy.

But someone is trying to destroy me and my business.

Hiring Callum Carmichael is my last chance to save it.

But I did not expect to fall for the grumpy giant.

Something about him makes my blood boil...and steam.

He's determined to knock down my walls.

I'm starting to think I want to let him.

If I survive the dangerous people determined to destroy me, anyway.

If you enjoy over-the-top bodyguards, fiery heroines, and steamy romance, you'll love this age-gap curvy girl romance!

CHAPTER ONE
Callum

"Siri, remind me to kill my cousin next time I see him."

"Adding *kill my cousin* to your schedule," my watch chirps. "Would you like to set a date and time?"

"No." I shake my head. *Jesus Christ.* "Siri, delete killing my cousin from my schedule before his wife strangles him, and I end up suspect *numero uno*." Bella threatens to kill my cousin, Cormac Carmichael, at least fifteen times a day since they got married a year ago. I am not getting my big ass tangled up in the middle of it when his crazy ass finally sends her over the edge.

Cormac, known around Silver Spoon Falls as Giant, is feral. He's been that way his entire life. He's never met a type of hell he didn't like to raise. Marriage hasn't settled him down at all. He goes out of his way to rile Bella up just so he can settle her down again. Bella isn't exactly tame herself. She has him wrapped around her little finger. They love each other fiercely. But if he ever goes missing, real talk, it'll be because she strangled him for driving her up the wall. His overprotective ass is bound to do it one of these days.

I drag my cell out of my pocket and dial his number.

"What's up, Callum?" His voice booms down the line on the second ring. One thing Cormac isn't is quiet. He's got one volume. Loud. "Are you already lost?"

"No, I'm not lost," I growl. "I could pee across town."

He laughs. "Then why are you calling me already?"

"I'm calling to tell you that I'm never doing you another favor ever again, asshole. Every single time I do, I live long enough to regret it." He and Bella—who he calls Mischief—are out of town with his MC for Daytona Bike Week and then they're spending a few days in Panama City before heading home, so he asked me to babysit a new client for him. He left out some pertinent details, though.

Like the fact that our new client owns the damn magic shop downtown—and I don't mean the kind where men pull rabbits out of hats. I'm talking about the one where they sell love poems and healing crystals alongside water bottled at one of the natural springs here in town. She calls the place *Hope Springs Eternal*.

"Grizz said you just left the office ten minutes ago. How could you possibly already regret it?" Cormac laughs at me. "Your ass hasn't even been there long enough to regret it."

"Oh yeah?" I open my camera app and click a photo of the front of the new client's storefront before shooting it to him. And then I immediately hit the button on the display to swap to the front-facing camera. I snap another photo—this time of my middle finger—and send it too. "Check your texts."

"Mischief was right. You do need to get laid."

"Tell Bella to stop worrying about my sex life." I swear to God, every time I come to town, the two of them gang up on me, trying to figure out why I'm still single. Truth is, I'm starting to wonder myself. I always told myself I'd make time to date eventually. But eventually never seems to come. Cormac and I run Carmichael Security, the private security firm our dads started when they were in their twenties. We've got branches in Tennessee, Texas, California, and New York. It doesn't leave a lot of time for much else.

I did not sign up to spend the week steeped in the Silver Spoon Falls water, though. Everyone in town swears it's magical or something. I guess they think the town has always been prosperous and residents are lucky in love because of it. I've seen enough since I've been coming here to know to drink the shit sparingly.

"You told me she had a store downtown," I mutter to Cormac when he sees my pictures and roars with laughter. "You didn't tell me she's the one who bottles and sells the fucking water to tourists, you asshole."

"You didn't ask."

I growl a string of curses, which only makes him laugh again.

"Suck it up, buttercup," he says. "It's only a few days. Besides, the job is legit. I guess someone has taken issue with the fact that Hope recently started selling the water and various remedies and tinctures. They've broken into her home twice, and someone ran her off the road two days ago. Until Dillon finds out who's behind the attacks, she needs protection."

"Hope. *Hope Springs Eternal*." I chuckle despite myself, impressed by the double play on words she managed to slip in there. And then I glance out the windshield of my truck at the little brick shop again. Crystals and gemstones of every sort line the front window. The name of the shop is painted across the glass, with the word springs situated inside a rendering of a fountain. Water and hearts spew from the top of it. The place seems harmless enough.

"I better not regret this," I mutter to Cormac.

"You won't."

I snort, not so sure I believe him. He's been saying the same thing since we were kids...usually right before he got me into ten kids of shit with my parents. Honestly, I'm surprised we survived half the dumb stuff we did back then.

"Good luck, fucker."

"Later." I stab the disconnect button and shove my phone back into my pocket. After another quick look at the shop, I haul my ass out of the truck to go introduce myself to Hope Byrne. The front door doesn't alarm or set off a bell when I open it. I make a note to fix that post haste. She needs to know when someone is entering the shop, especially if she's in danger.

I stop just inside the door, looking around.

"Jesus," I mutter. Mandalas and calming, happy colors hang everywhere alongside crystals and windchimes and shit I don't even have names for. Dried flowers and plants line shelves in jars, each labeled with their name and uses. It's all innocuous shit, things that make people feel as if they're taking charge of their lives, their health, and manifesting their own destinies. I'm sure there are plenty who don't see it that way though.

I wander through the shop for a full two minutes without seeing anyone.

What the fuck?

"Hello?" When no one answers, I circle around the counter, poking my head into the back. "Hello? Miss Byrne?" I call, and then wait for an answer. Twenty seconds later, one still hasn't come. I place my hand on the gun at the small of my back and slip down the short hallway leading into the back of the shop.

Pallets and boxes of water are stacked everywhere. A ceiling-high row of shelves on one wall holds more supplies, each arranged into various bins and buckets. The east wall contains what looks like a mixing station of some sort. Dried plants and flowers and little jars sit on a table beside measuring spoons and a chemist set. Everything is neat and tidy, making it clear Hope puts a lot of effort into running this place.

The middle of the room houses a giant packing station. Boxes and packing supplies are neatly arranged on top of folding card tables with a small tablet set up in the middle.

"Oh my gosh!" a woman cries from behind me.

I turn toward the sound of her voice and my cock stands up straight.

Hope Byrne is a curvy goddess. And she's not wearing anything but a pair of sheer blue panties.

CHAPTER TWO
Hope

I stare in shock at the sexy giant standing in the middle of my stockroom, staring at me like he wants to gobble me up. For a full five-count, neither of us moves. We just look at each other. His eyes climb up and down my body, lingering on my full breasts. They rake like fire down the swell of my belly, over my wide hips, and across the hot flesh between my legs. Even though I'm wearing panties, they don't exactly hide much.

He likes what he sees. His green eyes—the palest emerald I've ever seen—darken with desire. His tongue touches his full bottom lip. I shiver beneath the weight of his wanton gaze, turned on even though part of my mind recognizes this isn't at all how I should be reacting to a complete stranger seeing me mostly naked. Not even one who looks like this man.

Judging by the length of his hair, he isn't currently in the military, but I think he used to be. He's got that look to him—hard stare, rigid stance, built for war. The man's a ride as my granny would have bluntly stated.

Until he opens his mouth anyway.

"Where the fuck are your clothes?"

His rough growl finally breaks through the fog of lust addling my brain. My heart slams against my ribcage, jarring me into action. He broke into my store. He's in my stockroom where he has no business being. And I'm practically naked.

I shouldn't be standing here gaping. I need to protect myself.

"Get out!" I shout, grabbing the nearest thing in reach—a bottle of water—and launching it at him.

He snatches it out of the air like a freaking ninja, so I grab another one.

"Throw it and I'll spank your gorgeous ass," he warns me, his eyes narrowed.

I lower my arm, backing away from him. "If you came to hurt me, you'll live long enough to regret it." I inch toward the back door. Kieve is in the little courtyard out back, enjoying the morning sun. "I'm not alone."

"Liar. I just walked all through the store. You're the only one here."

"You sure about that?"

A flicker of hesitation crosses his face before he quickly schools his expression. "Why the fuck are you naked in the back of your shop with the front door unlocked, Hope?"

I don't ask how he knows my name. Everyone in Silver Spoon Falls knows everyone. Besides, my name is written across the front of my store since I opened it a few months ago.

"I didn't know the door was unlocked," I mutter under my breath, reaching behind my back for the door handle. At this point, I'm fairly sure he isn't here to hurt me, but he's being bossy and rude, so I'm not feeling particularly benevolent. As soon as my hand closes on the door handle, I yank it open. "Kieve, *tar anseo*!"

Kieve barks once and then comes flying through the door like a streak of lightning. He rushes straight for the sexy giant. My intruder jumps back a step as Kieve jumps around his feet, barking and growling like the wicked little beast he is.

"What the fuck?"

"Told you I wasn't alone."

"Call him off," he growls at me.

"Not until you leave."

"I'm definitely killing Cormac for this shit. He did not warn me you have a fucking guard dog." He bends down to scoop my Chihuahua up into his arms. "*Stad!*"

Kieve, the little traitor, immediately stops going crazy and settles down, his tongue lolling out.

I gape at him and the giant, my stomach sinking. He's Callum Carmichael, my new bodyguard? *Please, no.* "Cormac sent you?"

"Yep," he says, dashing my hopes all to pieces. His wild eyes roll over me. "Why don't you get dressed, and then we'll talk, Firefly?"

"Hope," I correct.

His lips curve upward. "Whatever you say, sweet Hope."

I narrow my eyes on him. "Can you at least turn around and stop staring at me?"

"Why? I've seen the show now." Those wild eyes rake down my body again. Heat courses through me, staining my cheeks red. "And god*damn*, Firefly. I'll be replaying it often."

"Oh, my God!" I stomp toward my tote, snatch it off the hook, and then flee to the privacy of the bathroom to change, which is what I was trying to do in the first place. I spilled coffee all over myself on my way in this morning because Kieve decided he wanted to chase a squirrel up a tree.

He never got the memo that he isn't a guard dog. I guess he thinks his police academy letter got lost in the mail. He's been extra vigilant since someone ran us off the road a couple of days ago. He trusts nothing and no one who isn't me. Except, apparently, Callum Carmichael.

I slam the bathroom door behind me, muttering under my breath about my traitor dog and Callum. The man is infuriating! And infuriatingly hot. There's no way I'm going to survive living with this man until Dillon Armstrong figures out who wants to destroy me and my business!

"You don't have a choice," I mutter to myself in the mirror, unzipping my tote bag to pull out the extra set of clothes I always leave here in case of emergencies. "Someone is trying to kill you."

The grim reminder sends a chill up my spine. I quickly yank my bra out of the bag and slip it on before yanking a sweater on over my head. It takes a minute to shimmy into the jeans. I think they shrank.

"Or my hips grew," I huff, out of breath by the time I get them on. Maybe it's time to stop sneaking next door to the coffee shop for breakfast every morning. The scones are addictive.

I fluff my hair, shove my coffee-stained clothes into the bag to take home to wash, and then slip my feet back into my ballet flats. My cheeks are still pink when I slip back out into the stockroom to face Callum.

I find him leaning against the wall with Kieve sitting at attention at his feet.

"Kieve, *imigh leat*," I murmur, pointing toward the front of the shop.

"He's well trained," Callum observes when Kieve immediately hops up and races toward the front of the shop.

I snort. "He's an adorable little terrorist is what he is."

"Chihuahuas usually are."

I drop the tote beside the packing station in the center of the room and then turn to face Callum, trying hard not to think about the fact that he's already seen me naked. "So you're Callum Carmichael."

"And you're Hope Byrne." His eyes do a slow drift over me, his gaze no less hotter than it was when I was mostly naked. "You never did answer my question, Firefly. Why the fuck are you running around your shop naked with your front door unlocked?"

"Okay, clearly we need to get a few things straight." I cross my arms to hide my boobs from his gaze. "First of all, I thought the door was locked. Secondly, I wasn't running around my shop naked. I stepped out of the bathroom to grab my bag so I could change. You're the one who decided you could just waltz right back here like you own the place—you don't, by the way. Third, I don't work for you. You don't get to bark questions at me like some hot drill sergeant and expect me to answer. This relationship will go a whole lot better if you get that through your thick head now. Fourth, stop calling me Firefly. My name is Hope."

He stares at me for a full ten seconds, not blinking. And then a devastating smirk overtakes his face. "Firefly suits you. You burn hot enough to light up the dark, baby."

My stomach turns a somersault. Lord, he's dangerous. And that has bad idea written all over it. I'm good at giving other people hope that real love and fairytale endings exist. I stopped believing in them myself when I was ten...the same day my dad killed my mom. I don't need this man trying to change my mind now.

"I'm not your baby, Callum. You're here to do a job. That's it."

"Fine. We'll do it your way."

For some reason, I don't think he means it.

Two seconds later, he confirms my suspicion.

"For now." He pushes away from the wall to stomp toward me, stopping when he's so close his cologne swirls in the air around me, clouding my senses with his rich, intoxicating smell. "But just so you know, the job ends as soon as your workday is over, Hope. Then, it's personal."

CHAPTER THREE
Callum

Hope and I don't get a chance to talk until noon. She does a surprising amount of local business. We make it to the front of the store just in time to rescue a young woman from Kieve. Locals trickle through the doors in a steady stream for the next few hours to chat, pick up cases of water, or browse the shop for crystals, gems, herbal teas, and a myriad of tinctures and remedies she sells. They seem to fall into two camps: the gray-haired denizens of town and those closer to her own age.

She has to lock Kieve behind the counter. Every time someone comes in, the dog goes berserk. He's a protective little monster. When no one else is around, he's chill. But as soon as someone steps through the front door, he turns into a pint-sized Cujo.

"Is he always like that?" I ask after he tries to bite an old man.

"No." Her shoulders droop. "He's been stressed out since someone tried to run us off the road a couple of days ago."

"He was with you?"

"He was my granny's dog before she passed," she says softly. "Now, he follows me everywhere. I don't go anywhere without him."

"You opened the shop a few months ago?"

"Three months ago."

"When did the attacks start?"

"Two and a half months ago."

My brows slash together. I was under the impression that the attacks just started, but they started immediately after she set up shop. "Someone wants to run you out of business."

"Someone wants to kill me," she mutters. "They weren't trying to scare me when they ran me off the road. They were trying to kill me."

"What makes you so sure?"

She lifts her gorgeous green eyes to mine. "They cut my brake line first." Fear turns her gaze stark, darkening the lush green of her irises and dilating her pupils. "Had I not hit another vehicle, my car would have plunged over the cliff into The Falls."

"Jesus." My hackles rise. I've been out to The Falls. It's a waterfall that plunges down into a small body of water on the outskirts of town. The cliff isn't necessarily high, but it's a big enough drop to seriously injure or kill someone, especially if they careen over it in a fucking car. Whoever tried to ensure she went over the edge wasn't trying to scare her. They were trying to hurt her. "Do you have any idea who would want to hurt you, Firefly?"

"No," she whispers, shaking her head. "I don't have any enemies. Neither did my granny that I know of. She died six months ago."

"Any family with a grudge?"

"It was just the two of us." She swallows, busying herself with a stack of receipts to avoid my gaze. "Um, my mom is dead, and my dad is in prison."

"How long?"

"Forever."

"What were his charges?"

"It doesn't matter. It was a long time ago, and he has nothing to do with this. He's in prison and isn't getting out so it wasn't him," she mutters, still refusing to look at me. "He'll never get out."

I push myself away from the wall where I've been standing and stride toward her, refusing to let her block me from her line of sight while we have this conversation.

Whatever she's ashamed of, it's not hers to carry. I plant myself directly in front of her, reaching across the counter to tip her chin up.

"Look at me, Firefly."

She resists for a long moment, willful and stubborn. She's going to be a handful, I already know. A thrill goes down my spine at the thought of teaching her to submit. I'm not a Dominant. I'm not into BDSM or any of that. But when she's in my bed—and she will be in my bed, I decided that as soon as I set eyes on her—she'll learn to obey. She'll learn to love it.

"Now, Hope," I demand, my voice firm.

"What?" she growls, twin spots of color turning her cheeks red as her defiant eyes flash to mine.

"What were his charges, Firefly?"

"It doesn't matter." It's a lie. I see the pain and grief in her eyes.

"Tell me."

She hesitates and then expels a sad sigh. "Murder, okay? He killed my mom."

I rock back on my heels, shocked. I suspected her to tell me the charges were murder. I did not expect for her to say he murdered her mom. Jesus. No wonder she doesn't want to talk about it. "How old were you, baby?"

"Ten."

I circle around the checkout counter to her, wrapping my hand around hers to tug her toward me. Kieve lifts his head from his bone to look at me and then decides his bone is more interesting than I am. I pull Hope toward me, not stopping until she's pressed up against my chest.

"Thank you for telling me," I murmur, pressing a soft kiss to her forehead.

"It's not like you gave me a choice," she complains.

"Didn't like the look on your face."

"What look?"

"Like you had something to be ashamed of." I tuck a strand of her honey and cinnamon hair behind her ear. "What he did is on him. The shame and guilt isn't your burden to carry and it doesn't reflect on you, Firefly."

"Tell that to my classmates," she snorts, slipping from my arms to put distance between us.

Fuck. They were mean to her about it, probably threw it in her face just to hurt her. Kids can be real assholes sometimes, especially to those with parents who do something awful. In a perfect world, children wouldn't suffer for the sins of the father, but this world is far from perfect. All too often, they suffer anyway. I think maybe Hope knows that better than anyone.

She's right, though. If her father is in prison for life, I doubt he's behind the attacks. He stands to gain absolutely nothing. Even if he were to automatically inherit her estate upon her death, he'd never see a penny of it, not while he's serving life in prison for murdering her mom. Which means he probably isn't our guy.

"I'm going to step out and make a few phone calls. Will you be all right in here by yourself for a little while, Firefly?" I watch as she fidgets around by the register, not really doing anything. She's just trying to avoid me. She's not used to being close to people. Or maybe it's that she's not used to being close to men. I don't know. But she's skittish, with walls built a mile high.

I intend to topple every one of them to the ground. I decided that approximately two minutes after meeting her. Looks like the water in this fucking town claimed another victim. Or maybe it's just Hope. I don't know. All I know is that her and her fiery spirit are mine.

"I'll be fine, Callum," she says. "Whoever keeps trying to get to me usually does it once I leave town. I guess they don't want to risk being seen."

"I'll be right outside. I'll have Grizz pick us up lunch when he drops off cameras and a bell for the door."

"Cameras?"

"You need security."

"I hired you."

I don't bother telling her that I'm not taking her money. I have a feeling it'll just piss her off. She's independent. "Eventually, you'll be on your own again, Hope," I murmur. "You need cameras so you can see what's happening out front while you're in the back and vice versa. You'll also be able to see Kieve in the courtyard to check on him. And a bell will alert you anytime the door opens."

"Fine." She throws up her hands. "Do what you want. I have a feeling you will anyway."

"Probably," I agree with a smile.

She narrows her eyes at me, muttering under her breath about bossy men who think they're the boss of her.

I chuckle and duck out of the shop, pulling my phone out of my pocket to call Dillon Armstrong. Green and gold St. Patrick's Day decorations flutter in the breeze all up and down the street, giving downtown a festive, bucolic air.

"This is Dillon," Armstrong growls on the second ring.

"It's Callum," I say. Dillon knows who I am. Even though Cormac runs the Texas branch of Carmichael Security, I've been spending more than my fair share of time here lately. Truth be told, Silver Spoon Falls just feels like home. The more I'm here, the more I want to be here. Cian and Corrin, our twin cousins, are back in Nashville. They're more than capable of handling shit there.

"What's up, Callum?"

"Hope Byrne," I state. "What do you know?"

"Figured I'd be hearing from you about her," he mutters. "Cormac warned me you were taking her as a client."

"Started today."

"We're running through a list of the usual suspects. She's well-liked in town. No one spoke out against her business when she applied for the licensing. She hasn't had any complaints about anything except her damn dog," he says, running down the list. "The best I can figure is the dispute is over her land but whoever wants it is trying to hide that by making it about the business."

"Why the land?"

"The mineral rights are worth a fortune. Her grandmother was approached multiple times to sell but refused. When she died, Hope ran off two different oil companies and God only knows who else."

"Jesus." I plaster myself against the side of the building as a young woman pushing a stroller jogs by. "You think one of them would send someone after her to try to hurt her?"

"Possibly. They've been pretty insistent from what she's told me," he says with a heavy sigh. "Ransom Oil has been sending their man around for months. I wouldn't be surprised if they tried to scare her into selling. They're hard up from what I've heard. But this rises beyond simply trying to scare her. Whoever is after her cut her brakes and rammed her car four different times. They were trying to kill her."

"Anyone get a look at the vehicle?"

"The driver of the SUV she hit swears it was an old white cargo van, but he didn't get a look at the driver. They fled the scene, heading out of town. I've been trying to run down every cargo van registered in the county, but there are a fucking ton of the bastards," he growls. "Romano International auctions off their used vans at the county auction every three years. They sell for cheap, so businesses and people in need of cheap transportation scoop them up quick."

"Fucking hell." Romano International is a massive company. They probably have fifty or sixty vans in their fleet at a time. If they're auctioning off used vans every three years, there are probably two hundred or more in the county. It'll take Dillon forever to chase them all down. "Keep me posted."

"Will do," he agrees. "I assume you'll be staying on the property with her?"

"That's the plan."

"Good. She's too goddamn stubborn to listen to reason. I tried to get her to come stay with me and Jules after the second break-in but she refused, said she isn't going to be scared out of her own home. She needs someone out there, though. Her nearest neighbor is as useless as tits on a fucking frog, and there's no one else for miles."

"I've got her now. She'll be fine."

Dillon hesitates and then he chuckles. "Well, goddamn. That was fast. I'm not sure if I should say congratulations or send my condolences."

"I'm hanging up now," I mutter, rolling my eyes. I swear to God, the men in this town can smell blood in the water. As soon as some poor bastard catches feelings, they start their shit. And I already know it'll be all over town by the end of the day. They gossip like high school girls. It's goddamn ridiculous.

"Later, you crabby bastard."

I grunt and then hang up on him. I'm not crabby. Just haven't had a reason to smile in a while. All I've fucking done for years is work. That'll be changing though. Once Hope is mine, I plan to spend a lot less time working and a lot more time following her around like her wicked little dog.

Just as soon as I figure out who the fuck is trying to hurt her and end them.

CHAPTER FOUR
Hope

"Great," I mutter, pulling into my driveway with Callum following behind me in his truck. Silas Wembley leans against the post on my front porch, his hands shoved into his pockets as he waits with his cowboy hat pulled down low over his face.

He owns the ranch next door. I think he has a thing for me, but that is never going to happen. Ever. He's in his late fifties. And he's so freaking pleasant about everything all the time. It's honestly exhausting. I like him well enough, don't get me wrong. He's been a lot of help around here, especially since Granny died. But the feelings are purely platonic.

I just don't really want to deal with him and Callum at the same time. It's already been a long day, and it's nowhere close to over. Until Dillon catches whoever is trying to ruin me and my business, Callum will be staying with me. In my house. In my space. How am I supposed to resist him when he's already wreaking havoc on my brain?

Every time I look at him, my heart races, and my stomach quivers. I think about the fact that he saw me practically naked, and my body catches on fire. He's supposed to be here to protect me, but I think I may need protection from him because he is dangerous on a whole new level.

Kieve growls as soon as he sees Silas, making me groan. He hates our neighbor.

"Behave," I warn him, pulling into the carport. "You can't just bite him every time he comes over, Kieve. It's rude."

Kieve gives me the side-eye, which I assume means mind my fluffing business.

I kill the engine and collect my bag and Kieve. By the time I reach for the door handle, Callum is already at my side, holding out a hand to help me out.

"Give me your stuff, Firefly," he says. "I'll carry it."

"I've got it."

"Firefly."

I huff and reluctantly hand it over, knowing arguing won't get me anywhere. He's bossy and he's a gentleman. It's an odd combination. I think I like it.

"Who's the douche on the porch?"

"Callum!" I hiss, shooting him a death glare when he says it loudly, as if to ensure Silas hears him.

"Answer the question, baby."

"Silas Wembley. He's my neighbor."

Callum grunts. "He come around a lot?"

"Sometimes," I lie, avoiding his gaze while I shove the door closed.

"Right." He waits for me to close the door, then follows me around the side of the house toward the front porch, walking so close I practically feel the tension radiating from him with every step.

"Howdy, neighbor." Silas jogs down the steps to meet us. He has a bright smile pasted on his face, but it doesn't quite reflect in his dark gaze as he looks Callum over. "I didn't realize you were going to have company today."

"Hi, Silas," I say, annoyed at the subtle chastisement in his tone, as if I did something wrong by not alerting him to my every move. "I didn't know you were coming over unannounced again."

"Presumptuous prick," Callum mutters under his breath.

Kieve barks once as if in agreement.

"Here, Firefly. Let me have him." Callum scoops him from my arms without waiting for my response. Naturally, Kieve doesn't bark or growl or snap at him. He and Callum are fast friends already. They glare at Silas together.

Silas stares at Kieve, the same bright smile pasted on his face. Irritated lines appear around his eyes though, making it clear he's jealous Kieve has taken to Callum but wants nothing to do with him. Silas can be...odd. Like a wounded deer. He never says anything, but he gets his feelings hurt easily. "The little guy finally made a friend, huh?"

"He knows who he can trust." Callum scratches Kieve's head.

"I'm sorry. I didn't catch your name."

"Didn't give it," Callum mutters, making it clear what he thinks about Silas with those three words. His gaze rolls over my neighbor and then he snorts before looking at me. "Do you want me to start dinner, baby?"

"Baby?" Silas says. "I didn't realize you were seeing anyone, Hope."

I'm going to murder Callum Carmichael. Slowly. Right after I kiss that smirk off his face. What? No. No, I am not kissing him.

"Silas, this is Callum Carmichael. Callum, Silas Wembley."

"Carmichael. You any relation to Cormac Carmichael?" Silas asks.

"Cousin."

"Good man," Silas says. "It's nice to meet you."

"Yeah," Callum agrees without returning the sentiment. He doesn't offer his hand to shake, either. He clearly does not like Silas at all.

"Good to know she'll have someone over here to watch out for her with everything going on," Silas says. "I know I'll sleep better at night knowing she's not out here alone and defenseless."

"Do you lose a lot of sleep thinking about her?" Callum growls.

Oh, good grief.

"It's been a long day, Silas," I quickly interject before he can answer. "Did you need something?"

"Your labels were delivered to my house again." His smile returns, brighter than ever. "I took the box out to your shop for you like the last one."

Again? That's the third one in a row. I don't know why the delivery service can't seem to get the address right. It's not like it isn't clearly printed on my mailbox and the house.

"Thank you," I sigh. "I'll call the carrier again tomorrow and try to get it sorted out again."

"It's not a problem."

Callum grunts.

I elbow him in the ribs this time.

"Well, I'll let you two get inside to your dinner." Silas glances from me to Callum. "If you need anything, Hope, you know where to find me."

"Thanks."

He steps around us, his boots thumping against the sidewalk as he takes off for his property. I wait until he's out of earshot to spin around to face Callum.

"Are you insane?" I whisper-hiss, glaring at him. "You can't just tell people that we're dating!"

"I didn't tell him that. He assumed." He smirks at me, his emerald eyes glowing with satisfaction. "And you didn't correct the assumption, Firefly."

"You...I..."

"You don't like him."

"He's fine."

"You want to rephrase that?" Callum growls, his smirk slipping as his voice deepens.

"What?" I gape at him for a moment, not sure what the heck he's talking about, and then it dawns on me and I roll my eyes. "I mean he's fine as a person, Callum. Jeez. I'm not attracted to him."

"Good."

"You were incredibly rude."

"Don't like him," he mutters, shrugging.

"You don't even know him!"

"I know he was waiting on your fucking porch for you. And I'm guessing it happens more often than you're going to admit. I'm also guessing your packages conveniently show up at his place a little too often too."

"That's not his fault."

"It is if he's making sure they're showing up at his place," he says. "Why does he have access to your shop?"

"Because it's easier for him to put the packages in there than for me to drag them out there," I mutter and then throw up a hand. "You know what? I did not sign up for the Inquisition when I hired you."

"Told you already, Firefly. The job ended when your workday did. It's personal now. Someone is trying to hurt you, and right now, he's the most likely candidate."

I gape at him for a full five count and then burst into laughter. "You think *Silas* is behind all of this? Good grief, Callum. You've lost your mind. The man wouldn't hurt a fly. He's obnoxious, but he has nothing to gain here."

"Except you and your land." He tips my chin up by crooking a finger beneath it. "You think you aren't a prize worth fighting dirty to get, Firefly? You're wrong. There's no limit to things I'd do to win you."

He means it. The truth glitters like the brightest stars in his eyes. He'd fight wars and topple kingdoms for me. He wouldn't hesitate or regret it, either. Lord. Who *is* this man?

I swallow my laughter, my mouth going dry.

"The only thing I'd never do is hurt you."

"Callum," I whisper, not sure if I'm asking him to kiss me or begging him not to break my heart. Both, I think. I want him with an intensity that scares the hell out of me. But can I take a taste of him without risking my heart?

No, a little voice whispers. *You know you can't.*

Kieve squirms in his arms, demanding to be let down. He holds my gaze as he stoops, carefully placing my dog on the ground. Kieve immediately takes off to explore the front yard. He won't go far. He knows not to leave the yard.

Callum rises to his full height, his eyes still locked on mine. "We've got a problem, Firefly," he murmurs, dropping my bag to the ground to tug me into his arms. "If I kiss you like you're practically begging me to do right now, it won't be enough to satisfy either one of us, and we both know it."

"T-that's a problem?"

"A big fucking problem," he growls, tilting his hips to press his erection against my lower belly. "I'm trying to make you my forever, not my for right now. I don't want to fuck it up, move too fast, and lose you for good."

"Callum," I whisper, my heart beating so loud I'm sure he can hear it. Anxiety courses through me, urging me to back away, to throw up walls to keep him at a distance. He's getting too close to dangerous territory, to the place where happily-ever-after ends with little girls growing up without parents. But he isn't my dad. I'm not my mom. And their story doesn't have to be ours.

I can't run scared forever. Eventually, I have to let someone in. I have to face my fears and learn to trust. I think...I think I want that person to be Callum. Something about him calls to me. It has all day. The way he looks at me. The way he speaks to me. For the first time, I want to know what it's like to just let go of the fear and just...feel.

"Kiss me," I plead. "I won't regret it."

He spears his hand into my hair, dragging my mouth to his with a needy groan I feel in my bones. His lips touch mine, soft at first. Electricity sparks between us, humming to life like livewires. He feels it too. He groans again and pulls me closer, his hand tightening in my hair.

His tongue flicks against my bottom lip, demanding entry. I give it to him, willingly opening to him. I whimper as he sweeps inside, tangling his tongue with mine. As soon as his strokes against mine, I lose the ability to think. My legs tremble, my knees threatening to buckle.

"Fuck." He releases my hair to drag me closer to his body as my legs give out altogether. "This perfect mouth is going to ruin me."

His already ruined me. He's ruining me with it right now.

His hands prowl down my body, gripping my ass in his palms to pull me even closer. He doesn't handle me like I'm delicate. He handles me like I'm his, holding onto me as if he's not planning to let go anytime soon. The possessive edge to his touch is the single sexiest thing I've ever experienced.

"Callum," I moan into his mouth, pleading for a taste of the forbidden.

He gives it to me when he breaks from my mouth to kiss a trail down my chest. Right there on the sidewalk in front of the house, his mouth closes over my right breast, and his teeth around my nipple. He bites me, shoving his knee between my legs to grind me down on it at the same time.

I turn to putty in his arms, throwing my head back to shout his name into the sky as lava flows through my veins in place of blood. It feels so good. God, I feel like I'm flying even though my feet haven't even left the ground.

"Oh, Firefly," he groans, kissing his way back to my mouth. He nips my bottom lip before brushing a sweet kiss across the bite. "When I get inside you, I'm going to ruin us both."

I'm pretty sure he ruined me already.

CHAPTER FIVE
Callum

After dinner, Hope leads me out to her shop to show me around. The shop itself is a large metal building situated beside a natural spring on the property. The bottling machine is a massive contraption that takes up half the shop. Empty bottles hang from one end. Full bottles fill a pushcart on the other, with a table full of labels and shrink-wrap packaging a little farther away.

"Water is pumped in through here," she explains, pointing out the lines running to the spring outside the building, "where it's filtered and purified, and then bottles are filled automatically before moving down the line to be labeled and packaged. All I have to do is place the bottles on the line to be filled and then pull them off the end, label, and pack." Her nose wrinkles. "And keep an eye out to make sure nothing gets jammed up. The caps get stuck sometimes."

"You do all this by yourself?"

"Two high school students help label and pack on weekends, but otherwise, yeah, it's just me and Betty here." She pats the side of the machine affectionately. "We do okay by ourselves."

"It's a lot of fucking work, Firefly."

"Eventually, I'll be able to hire full-time help," she says quietly. "But it's not in the budget yet. The first three months have been amazing, but I have a long way to go before I'm to that point."

"Why sell the water?"

"Why not?" She shrugs. "This land has been in my family for generations. I grew up listening to my granny tell me stories about how special the water is here. I've spent most of my life listening to people in town talk about it the same way. To everyone outside of Silver Spoon Falls, it's just water. But to the people here, it means something. It's hope and a connection to the land and our past. It's the thing that allowed us to survive when so many others weren't as fortunate. They believe in it because everyone needs a little magic in their lives. It's what keeps us young."

"You don't believe it."

"I don't know what I believe anymore," she whispers, looking at me through her lashes with a troubled expression. "It's hard to believe in fairytales and happily-ever-after when the only example I had growing up ended the way it did. But...I don't know. Maybe I bottle it because I want to believe."

Poor little firefly. She aches to know what love feels like, but is terrified to reach for it. The memories from her past are burned into her psyche, making her hesitant to trust even her own heart. I'm going to change that. I'm going to teach her that she can trust what it's telling her. She can trust me.

Our love story won't end like her parents did. I won't ever allow that. I don't want to harm this fiery goddess. I want to worship at her feet. That's what a king does. Worships his queen. Protects her. Defends her above all others. She doesn't know me well yet, but she will. I'm not just going to be her bodyguard. I'm going to be the reason her heart beats...the one person she trusts with every little piece of herself.

I stride toward her, tipping her chin up until her gorgeous eyes meet mine. "I'm going to make you believe, sweet Hope," I murmur before brushing my lips across hers in a soft pass. I want to deepen the kiss, take more. Always, I want more of her.

She's sparked a hunger in my soul that nothing short of possessing her will sate. But now isn't the time for that. Baby steps. Even if it fucking kills me. And just so we're clear, it very well might kill me. My dick has never been this hard before...and it's been this hard all goddamn day.

I reluctantly pull back before I can take too much or get lost in her. It's far too easy to do when she burns as hot as she does. She goes up like kindling as soon as I get her in my arms. But now isn't the time. "What can I do to help?"

"You want to help?" She arches a brow at me, looking at me like I've lost my mind. "I thought you said your job ended when my workday did."

"I did, but your workday clearly isn't over." I'm guessing her workday rarely ever ends if she's running this operation by herself. She probably works herself to the bone trying to do it all. Her shop may be new, but it was busy all day. People in town love that she's selling local water. It's a huge hit. And the fact that she's made it available online means she isn't just selling to locals through her shop. She's got online customers, businesses, and God only knows who else she has to worry about too. "Teach me how to work Betty."

"You want to operate Betty?"

"There you go again with the surprise." I turn her toward the machine, tapping her on the ass. "Less of that. More instruction, Firefly. We've got shit to do."

For the next two hours, she loads bottles into the front end of the machine, and I haul full bottles off the other end. By the time we shut down the machine, we've amassed a mountain of full bottles, and I'm fucking exhausting. It's back-breaking work.

I'm in awe of the fact that she's been doing this shit by herself for the last three months. As soon as she's mine, I'm hiring someone to help her. There's no way she should be doing this alone every day. I'm three times her size and my arms feel like Jell-O.

"Wow." She gapes at the mountain of full bottles. "I've never gotten that many done at a time before. Sam and Ethan are going to hate me this weekend."

"Sam and Ethan?"

"The kids who label and package," she says, smiling over at me. "Thank you, Callum. It would have taken me all week to get this much done on my own."

"You can thank me by taking your sexy ass in the house and soaking in a bubble bath, Firefly." I prowl toward her before dragging her into my arms to steal a kiss. I can't help it. Her cheeks are flushed. Tendrils of hair stick to her face where she's all sweaty. She's too fucking beautiful.

Her arms wind around my neck as she anchors her body to mine. I palm her curvy ass, trying to get my fill while I can since I already know she isn't going to let me sleep in her bed tonight. She'll kick my ass if I even suggest it. But that's what I want...for her to fall asleep in her arms, her head on my chest.

I'm falling hard. I didn't even stand a chance with her. She appeared naked in her shop and pulled the rug out from under me. I landed flat on my back, staring up at heaven. Didn't know it was five-foot eight with honey and cinnamon hair, ocean eyes, and curves for days. But it looks like that's exactly where my heaven begins and ends. With her.

"Callum," she whispers against my lips, running her fingers through the hair at the nape of my neck. "You have to stop kissing me. You're going to get me addicted."

'That's the plan, Firefly."

"I knew you were going to say that."

"Do you want me to slow down?"

"I...No," she says, her voice a mere scrap of sound. "Just don't let me fall. Please?"

"We'll fall together, Firefly." I glide my nose against hers, groaning at how intimate it feels. "And when we land, you'll land in my arms. Deal?"

"Okay," she whispers, her breath sweet against my lips.

I kiss her again before reluctantly pulling back. We exit the shop together, her hand in mine. "Tell me about the oil company that's been hounding you about buying the property."

"How do you know about that?"

"Dillon told me."

"Of course he did," she mumbles, making me smile. She's not really annoyed with him. I just don't think she likes not being in control. She's been on her own for far too long. She doesn't know what it means to let herself be cared for. She's used to calling the shots and doing it all on her own.

"Tell me about them, Firefly."

"What do you want to know? They've been after the land for years, but I promised my granny that I wouldn't let them have it. I guess they thought I'd be easier to convince than she was," she says with an indelicate snort. "Their annoying little henchman quickly learned that isn't the case."

"He come around often?"

"Not since I threatened to shoot him next time he showed up out here."

I stop walking mid-step, turning to her in surprise.

"He was giving me a headache," she mumbles, avoiding my gaze. "He talks in circles about profits and losses and taxes and math things that annoy me. And I had a cheese-cake in the fridge calling my name."

"Jesus Christ." I laugh quietly. "What's his name?"

"Thomas Huntington."

"You think his company is behind the attacks?"

"Probably," she sighs heavily. "Others have been out here, asking me to sell, but they aren't nearly as insistent as Huntington and Ransom Oil have been. They really want my land. Probably because their stocks are tanking. The last few wells they put up in the area didn't do well."

"Why are they so sure yours will?"

"You mean you don't know?" She blinks wide eyes at me like a little owl in the dark. "Granny and Pa struck oil on the property way back in the sixties when they were digging a reservoir."

"They never did anything with it?"

Hope shakes her head. "They didn't care about the oil. Pa was a farmer. He didn't want anyone out here stripping the land to mine it for oil. When he died, Granny made sure she kept her promise to him." Her eyes flash in the dark, her expression fierce. "I intend to keep my promise too. They can have the oil over my dead body."

I growl at her words, getting all up in her personal space. "No one is going to hurt you to get your land, Hope," I vow, my protective instincts roaring at the thought. If Huntington and Ransom Oil are trying to kill her to get her property, they picked the wrong woman. This one is mine. I'll destroy their fucking company myself before I let them harm her.

But I'm not convinced it's them, not yet. Silas Wembley was a little too fucking comfortable showing up here un-invited. Hope may not have noticed the way he looked at her, but I sure as fuck did. The bastard is in love with her or thinks he is, anyway. Would he put her through all of this just so he could play her hero? Maybe. It wouldn't be the first time someone did something nine shades of fucked up to try to push someone into their arms.

I'll run his name and Huntington by Dillon tomorrow and see what he has to say. I'll also ask Finn Taylor, a close friend of Cormac's to look into Ransom Oil and Silas. If there's anything to find, Finn will find it. There's nothing he can't do with a computer.

"Come on, Firefly." I lace my fingers through Hope's, pulling her toward the house again. "That bubble bath is calling your name."

Chapter Six

Callum

I'm nearly asleep when glass shatters downstairs, bringing me wide awake. I sit bolt upright in the bed, reaching for the gun I tucked inside the nightstand beside me. I grab my cell with the other, shooting a quick text to Grizz.

Me: 911. Send back-up to Hope's.

I don't explain the situation. I don't have to explain. He's worked personal security long enough to know that a 911 text means act now, ask questions later. He's good people.

I climb from the bed as soon as I'm done typing the text, and stride toward the bedroom door, moving on silent feet. I don't turn on lights. Don't need them. I slip through the dark like a ghost, moving silently as I make my way across the hall to Hope's bedroom.

"Don't shoot me, Firefly," I breathe into the dark when Kieve growls a soft warning at me, alerting me to the fact that they're already awake. I'm guessing my girl was awake as soon as she heard the glass break. I'm also guessing she's armed.

Hope isn't a delicate little flower. She's more than capable of taking care of herself. She's a queen. But she has me now. She doesn't have to handle anything alone, especially not some motherfucker breaking into her house.

"Callum?" she whispers.

"You and Kieve stay here, Firefly. I've got back-up on the way."

"You can't go out there alone." The tremor in her voice breaks my fucking heart. How many times has she been through this alone? Scared as hell, but facing it on her own? Whoever is out there better fucking pray I don't catch them.

"Stay here, baby. Don't make me spank your gorgeous ass," I warn her before slipping out of the door without waiting for a response. We'll spend all night arguing if I let her. She doesn't take orders. Not yet. She'll learn eventually to give up a little of that control she clings to with both hands.

I slip down the hall, listening for any little sound, but none come. Where did the breaking glass come from? The living room? Kitchen? I don't know. I creep down the stairs, my gun aimed low.

The nightlight in the living room allows me to clear the room quickly before moving into the dining room. I nearly have a fucking heart attack when my reflection appears in the reflective glass of the china cabinet.

"Jesus fucking Christ," I whisper to myself before moving into the kitchen. Glass litters the floor beneath the back door where a rock was thrown through it, but it's still locked. I carefully clear the room, checking the pantry, the mudroom, and the laundry room anyway.

There's no one in the house.

I unlock the back door and step outside. My balls immediately threaten to crawl back into my body to hide. The temperature plunged in the last few hours. Silvery storm clouds roil overhead. Wind whips through the treetops, sending a chill wind whistling across the property. It's chilly as fuck outside.

I grit my teeth and carefully walk around the house anyway, scanning for intruders or any tracks. There are boot prints in the mud a few yards from the back door, but they end abruptly after a few feet. Whoever threw the rock did it and ran. I don't think they were trying to get in. They were trying to scare her.

Well, it fucking worked. She's scared. And I'm pissed.

"Callum?"

I spin around to find Hope standing at the door with a gun in her hands, her robe tied tightly around her waist. Her hair is wild, her eyes wide in her pale face.

"Did you find anything?"

"You were supposed to wait for me, Firefly."

"I was worried about you," she whispers.

How can I be mad when she's so fucking sweet?

"I didn't find anyone." I move toward her, my gun aimed at the ground. "I still need to check the shop though. Can you please wait inside while I do that?"

"They didn't get in the shop."

"How do you know that?"

"There's an alarm."

I back her into the kitchen before gently taking her handgun from her and placing it on the counter. I set mine beside hers before turning back to her, my heart pounding against my ribcage as my blood pressure rises. "You have an alarm on the shop, but not on the house," I state, staring at her levelly. "Is that what you're telling me?"

"Y-yes?" She gulps.

"Silas Wembley has the alarm code?"

"Yes."

"Where's your phone?"

She pulls it from her pocket.

"Change it, Firefly. Now."

"What? Callum, I don't think–"

"You want to trust him because that's who you are," I growl, cutting her off. "But I know what's standing in front of me right now. I know what I'd risk to keep you to myself. And I saw the way he looked at you today, Firefly.

He wants you, and I don't know how far he's willing to go to get you. Until I know the answer to that question, he doesn't get access to your shop, the house, or you. Period."

"W-what would you risk, Callum?"

"Everything," I snarl, dragging her into my arms. "I'd risk fucking *everything* to keep you to myself, Hope." My mouth closes over hers, my kiss hot and insistent. I don't give her a chance to say anything else. I consume her, worried as fuck that he has access to her shop. Maybe I'm just a jealous asshole. I don't fucking know. But she's mine. I'll do whatever I have to do to make sure she's safe, even if it means ensuring no one else ever gets close.

By the time Grizz and Dillon roll up in the driveway ten minutes later, Hope has changed the alarm code, and we've both thrown clothes on. I meet them on the front porch, leaving Hope inside with Kieve, who is riled up.

"What happened?" Dillon demands, jogging up the sidewalk toward me. Grizz is hot on his heels, his expression dark.

"Someone threw a rock through the kitchen door." I scrub a hand through my hair, cursing up at the sky. Rain already falls in fat, cold drops, a precursor to what's to come. It's supposed to rain all week. "They were gone before I got downstairs. Left boot prints out back."

"Son of a bitch," Dillon growls. "You see anything?"

"Nothing. Neither did Hope. I still need to check the shop. Figured one of you could help me clear it."

Dillon's brows furrow. "She didn't have the alarm set?"

"Oh, she had it set. But she isn't the only one with the alarm code." I shoot a dirty look at him. "You failed to tell me that her goddamn neighbor is basically stalking her."

"Stalking her?" Dillon's eyebrows climb toward his hairline. "You mean Silas?"

"The fucker was standing on her front porch when we got home today. Apparently, he finds a reason to stop by most days." I'm still pissed about it. "Didn't seem thrilled when he found out that she has a man."

Dillon's lips curve into a grin. He shakes his head, chuckling. "Silas is harmless, Callum. He's lived next door her whole life. Aithne Walsh asked him to keep an eye on Hope before she died. That's all he's doing."

"If you believe that bullshit, I've got oceanfront property in Arizona to sell you," I mutter. He's keeping an eye on her all right. But it's not because her grandma asked him to do it. The old bastard wants in her pants. If I'm too old for her—and I refuse to think about the fact that she's only twenty-four to my thirty-nine—then he's way too fucking old for her. Doesn't change the fact that he wants her.

"I'll look into him," Dillon sighs, shaking his head.

I grunt my appreciation. "Look into Thomas Huntington while you're at it. That's the name of the fucker Ransom Oil keeps sending around here," I mutter, stomping down the steps to lead him and Grizz out to the shop so we can check it. "Hope ran him off the property with a shotgun last time he was out here. Told him the only way they were getting the property was over her dead body."

"Jesus Christ," Grizz says, laughing abruptly. "Maybe Cormac should hire her."

I shoot him a glare. He just grins at me, unperturbed.

"Just saying. She's a badass."

"A badass likely to get herself killed," Dillon mutters, his tone dark. "She failed to mention any of this when she filled me in about Ransom Oil."

Why am I not surprised? I should spank her infuriating little ass. But truthfully, I expected nothing less. There's no way she was going to admit to the sheriff that she pulled a gun on Huntington. And I'm guessing she never considered that telling him the only way they were getting the property was if she were dead was like waving a flag in front of a bull. She's too goddamn innocent.

I unlocked the shop to check inside while Dillon and Grizz walk the perimeter, checking to make sure no one fucked with anything outside. I type in the new alarm code

Hope set—her grandfather's birthday—and then make a circuit. As far as I can tell, everything is exactly like we left it.

And yet...and yet something feels off. I check around Betty carefully, looking everything over, but find nothing. I poke through the boxes of packing supplies and the pile of bottles with the same results. There's nothing out here.

Shit, maybe I just need to own the fact that I'm a jealous asshole. I don't like Silas because he wants what belongs to me, plain and simple. Doesn't make him responsible for any of the shit going on around here.

Dillon and Grizz stick around long enough for Dillon to take photos of the door, collect the rock, and give us a report number, and then they head out. I expect an 'I told you so' when they leave, but Hope simply walks into my arms, snuggling up against my chest.

"I'm glad no one got in the shop," she whispers around a yawn. "Betty was expensive. I don't want anyone breaking her."

"I asked Grizz to get someone out here tomorrow to install cameras. We're going to put a few outside the shop and the house to help keep an eye on things. We're also going to put up motion lights." I run my hands through her hair. "I'll look into getting an alarm company out here this week to get the house wired up."

"I can't afford all of this, Callum."

"Did I say I was charging you, Firefly?"

"You can't just spend that kind of money on me. Are you insane?" She pulls back to look at me like I've lost my mind. "Cameras and alarms and motion lights cost a fortune. I know because I looked!"

Well, damn. Guess I can't tell her that they're cheap then.

"I can afford them, Hope." I snort. "I could buy cameras and alarms and motion lights every fucking day for the next five years and still be fine."

"Great," she groans. "You're rich too."

I chuckle, pressing my lips to her forehead. "Try to contain your enthusiasm there, Firefly."

She rolls her eyes at me. "I just mean, of course you're basically the perfect man. Well, except for the fact that you're bossy. And grumpy. And you never listen. And you're paranoid. And I think maybe you're also crazy, but the jury is still out on that one." She bites her lip, looking up at me. "Never mind. Maybe you aren't so perfect."

I growl playfully, snatching her up into my arms.

She laughs, throwing her arms around my shoulders. "I was just kidding."

"No, you weren't. You were being honest." It's what I love about her...that honesty. She doesn't mince words or tell me what she thinks I want to hear. She tells me exactly what she thinks. A lot of women would fall all over themselves after hearing that I have money. Not Hope. She bitches about it.

"I don't need your money, Callum. I don't want it. I hired you to do a job, not to spend money on me," she frets as I carry her upstairs with Kieve following behind.

"I'll make you a deal."

"What kind of deal?" Her eyes narrow on me. "And before you say anything, you should know that I have a shotgun in my bedroom if you suggest sleeping with you in exchange for money."

"No. What the fuck?" I scowl at her. "When you sleep with me, it won't be as part of any deal, Firefly. It'll be because you can't stand the thought of not having me fucking you raw a second longer," I say, holding her gaze. "Sex won't be a transaction between us. It'll be a revelation."

"Okay," she whispers, her expression softening. "What's your deal then?"

"Sleep with me."

"*An áit thíos atá ceapaithe duit, a dhiabhal*," she growls. I only understand about half of the fiery words as she spits them at me with her eyes shooting off sparks, but I'm pretty sure she just told me I belong in hell. She's probably right, but not this time.

"I meant *sleep*, Firefly. As in sleep in the bed with me. Get your mind out of the gutter." I shake my head, smiling. Goddamn. Her temper makes my dick hard as a rock. I can't wait until she unleashes it on me when she's naked beneath me and at my mercy. "I'm not trying to get you naked. I just want you where I know you'll be safe."

She eyes me suspiciously, those green eyes narrowed.

"Scout's Honor."

"If you were a Boy Scout, I'm a supermodel," she snorts, relaxing in my arms.

"Well, damn. Guess I better get your autograph now then."

CHAPTER SEVEN
Hope

I wake up with Callum's hard body wrapped around me, his erection digging into my back. One hand splays across my chest. The other is between my legs, cupping my center in a possessive hold. As soon as my eyes flutter open, my body temperature rises toward volcanic levels.

Callum Carmichael is in my bed.

His hand is between my thighs.

I bite my lip, trying not to moan out loud. Even though I shouldn't, I wriggle. I can't help it. I want to know what it feels like for him to touch me where no one else ever has. I ache to know what it's like to feel his fingers against my sex, pressing deep.

"Firefly." His voice is a gritty rasp against my ear. "Are you trying to get yourself into trouble this morning?"

"M-maybe."

He palms my breast, flicking one hard nipple as his teeth close around my earlobe. "Then be a fucking good girl and stay still for me," he growls in my ear. "Because if you don't, I'm going to flip you onto your stomach and fuck my kid into you right here and now."

"Callum," I moan, a wave of heat blasting through me at his wicked threat.

He yanks my panties to the side, running his fingers over my wet slit. "You've been grinding that gorgeous ass against me all fucking night long. Do you know how sweet you sound moaning my name in your sleep, Firefly?"

I was moaning for him in my sleep? Oh my God. I don't remember my dreams. All I remember is him. He was everywhere, heating me like metal on a forge. Driving me crazy. Even in my sleep, my body reacted to him. Even in my sleep, I wanted him. Even asleep...I think I'm falling for him.

What is he doing to me?

"Playing with my pussy," he breathes, using his thumb to part my folds. "And just so we're clear, this is all mine, Firefly. Every pretty little inch. Every drop you spill. All of it."

"Callum, please."

"Please, what?"

"Stop teasing me and claim it!" I cry, turned on, frustrated, and impatient. If he wants it, it's his. I'm not stopping him. I'm not telling him no. All signs point to freaking yes. Just, for the love of all that's holy, make me come before the ache swallows me whole.

His teeth close around the shell of my ear, delivering a sharp bite. He yanks my leg back over his hip at the same time, opening me up to him. As soon as I'm where he wants me, he delivers a little slap to my center. His hand lands against me with a wet smack.

I shout his name, my hips arching toward his hand.

"Learn to give it up, Hope."

"G-give what up?"

"Control. Give it to me." His fingers dance around my folds again, so close to where I need them, but not nearly close enough. He's tormenting me, refusing to give me what I want until I give him what he wants. He's going to keep me right here on the edge until I cede control, willingly allowing him to slip into my soul.

I resist, not because I want to do it, but because I think he likes it when I fight him. He likes that I don't give him what he wants as soon as he demands it. He may want control, but he wants to earn it just as much as I need him to earn it. I don't trust easily, but with this man? I could easily fall for him, fall *into* him. Already, I teeter on the edge, mere centimeters from falling headfirst into something vast and terrifying.

I won't just hand him my heart. I'll give him my soul.

"Goddamn, Firefly. You drive me fucking crazy." His teeth rake down the side of my throat, his scruff abrading my sensitive skin. He slips his hand beneath my shirt to roll one nipple between his fingers. "Do you want me fucking you here and now? Is that it?"

"Callum." I writhe in sweet torment, pleading for mercy. My body bows as I submit to him, giving him the control he craves. I don't care what he does to me in this moment just so long as he doesn't stop. "Please. Oh God, please."

"That's it," he croons. "Let me take care of you. You think I won't? Fuck no, Firefly. When you're in my arms, you'll never go unsatisfied." His thumb touches my clit as one finger circles my opening. "Pleasing you will be my motherfucking goal in life."

I claw at his arms as he slowly presses his thick finger inside me, grinding his thumb against my clit at the same time. The dichotomy of sensations is too much. I'm full and not full enough, burning for more even as pleasure bubbles through my system, popping in my veins.

"Callum, I'm...I'm..."

"Fall, Firefly," he breathes against my ear, thrusting his finger in and out of me as his thumb grinds against my clit again and then again. "I'll catch you." His lips close around the pulse hammering in my throat. His fingers close around my nipple.

I shatter apart in his arms, crying his name into the room. I fall into him, trusting him to catch me like he promised he would.

He doesn't let me down.

It's the closest to real magic I've ever come.

It's the closest to perfect I've ever felt.

"Stop looking at me like that."

"Like what?"

"Like that!" I cry, hiding my face in my hands as he smirks at me from the driver's seat of his truck an hour later.

His wicked laugh rolls over me, making my stomach quiver.

I split my fingers apart to peek at him from between them. He's still wearing the same grin he's been wearing all morning. He looks like a little boy who got into the cookie jar. That crooked smirk is far too sexy on him.

"Pay attention to the road before you get us killed," I demand, pulling my hands from my face when a crack of lightning splits the sky open. It's storming like crazy. Whoever said tornadoes have a season lied. Around here, any season is tornado season if Mother Nature wills it so.

I'm just praying it's been too cold for her to will it to be today. I have work to do.

"I'd never risk your life, Firefly." He shoots me a reproachful look.

"I know." I reach across the console of his truck to squeeze his muscular forearm in reassurance. How can I doubt him? He wouldn't even let me drive myself to work this morning because of the rain. He was worried about me and Kieve. "I was just teasing."

We drive in silence the rest of the way to my shop downtown. Instead of pulling into the parking lot, Callum pulls right up to the front door and then hops out before circling around to my side to help me and Kieve out.

"You go in out of the rain, Firefly. I'll carry your shit inside."

It's such a small thing, but the gesture makes my heart flutter. I don't know where this man came from or how he ended up in my path. I don't think I did anything to deserve him. But, please God, can I keep him?

I secure a grumbling Kieve under one arm to unlock the door and then hurry through out of the rain. Even though there's an awning over the door, it's not doing much good with the wind whipping rain every which way out there.

My foot slips on a piece of paper that was shoved through the mail slot. I bend down to set Kieve on his feet and pick it up, not even looking at it before I hurry to disarm the alarm system.

Kieve jumps up on the door, looking out at the rain. He whines softly.

"Sorry, little guy. There's nothing I can do about it. You'll just have to hang out in here with us today," I tell him, moving to the counter to drop my keys and the flyer that was in the floor. Only when I lay it on the counter, I see my name written across the top in a messy scrawl.

Hope

You were warned but you continue to defy. Consider this your final chance to save yourself. Close up shop and stop selling the water and your witchcraft. You won't like what comes next.

My hands shake as I read the note, bile climbing up my throat. Hot tears sting my eyes, but I refuse to let them fall. Whoever is doing this doesn't deserve my tears, not even angry, defiant ones.

The bell over the front door chimes. I nearly jump out of my skin.

"It's raining like a motherfucker out there," Callum mutters, and then catches sight of my face. His expression turns stony. He's across the shop to my side in three steps. "What happened?"

I hold the letter out toward him, hating the way my hands tremble.

"Son of a bitch." He drops the letter, dragging me into his arms. "They aren't going to get close to you, Firefly. I'll destroy anyone who fucking tries." Pure murder seethes in his tone, vibrating just below the surface.

"It's not witchcraft," I mumble. "The poems I sell with the water aren't spells. They're just kitschy love poems. The crystals and gemstones and remedies...all of those are things my family brought over from Ireland. My grandpa grew most of the flowers and herbs. My granny taught me how to mix the salves and ointments. It's herbal remedies, that's it."

"I know, baby. I know."

"I don't understand why someone is doing this. Why do they hate me so much? I'm just trying to survive. Is that so wrong?"

"Fuck no," he rasps in my ear, tilting my head back until my watery eyes meet his. "You don't deserve any of this, Hope. Whoever is doing it isn't doing it because you deserve it. It's not because of anything you sell in this shop or because of who you are. It's because of what they want from you. They're trying to break you down so you have nowhere to turn except to them."

Would Silas really do all of this just because he has a thing for me? I can't imagine it...but maybe that's because I don't *want* to imagine it. I've known him since I was ten years old. The fact that he has a crush on me makes my skin crawl, but I never thought he was dangerous. Maybe I just didn't see it, though. Maybe I'm just as blind as my mom was.

Or maybe it is Thomas Huntington, trying to force me into selling my land. If he takes my business from me, I won't have a choice but to sell. Is he the one trying to destroy me? Would his company go that far to get my family's land? I don't know.

"They miscalculated, Firefly." Callum runs his thumb across my bottom lip, his expression soft. "Whoever it was thought they could scare you into running to them, but you don't break easily. You don't scare easily. You don't need anyone to save you. You save yourself."

He's right...but he's wrong too.

"I've always relied on myself. I didn't have a choice." I swallow the lump in my throat. "My granny was diagnosed with terminal liver disease when I was fourteen. The first few years were okay. She didn't need much help. But by the time I finished high school, I took care of her more than she took care of me. There wasn't anyone else to step in and do it. We barely scraped by, but we made it.

"Her life insurance helped ensure I wouldn't end up on the streets. I was able to pay her medical bills, buy Betty, and lease the shop downtown. If I lose it, I'll lose everything, Callum." Tears well in my eyes, spilling over. "That's why I went to Cormac. This time, I can't save myself."

"You don't have to, Hope." He cups my cheeks, collecting the tears that spill down my cheeks with the pads of his thumbs. "I'm right here, and I'm not going anywhere.

They can't break you. I'll crawl through hell before I allow that to happen."

I want to ask why he's willing to fight so hard for me...but I already know the answer to that question. It's right there in his eyes, reflecting back at me like stars.

He's in love with me.

CHAPTER EIGHT
Callum

Once Hope calms down, she retreats to the stockroom to get some work done while I start going through the security camera footage to see what I can find. I also call Dillon so he can send someone over to pick up the note. He tells me to put it aside, stop touching it, and he'll be here to get it before noon.

I texted Finn before we left the house to ask him to look into Silas and Huntington. Since his wife is eight months pregnant, they didn't go to Daytona with the rest of the MC. His office isn't far from here, so he said he'd stop by this morning so we can talk. I'm still going through the camera footage when he raps on the door.

I pause the video feed and scoop Kieve up from the floor before strolling to the door to let him in. The shop won't open for another hour, but Hope works her ass off. She's here early every day to package orders that need to be mailed out to online customers and do the eighty other things that come with running a business.

Kieve growls at Finn when he ducks through the door into the shop, cursing when his glasses immediately fog up. He pulls them from his face, eyeing the little dog in my arms with a shit-eating grin.

"A Chihuahua?"

"He thinks he's a goddamn Malinois," I mutter, scratching behind his ears. "Don't try to pet him. He may try to take a finger off."

Finn chuckles, glancing around the shop. "Been wondering what the fuck was in here. Scarlett is fascinated by all the crystals in the window. Aithne's granddaughter owns the place, right?"

I don't bother to ask how he knows that. Even if this weren't Silver Spoon Falls where everyone knows everyone, Finn would know. Every damn governmental agency from here to Japan has tried to hire him at one point. He can hack his way into anything.

"Yeah, Hope." I carry Kieve across the shop and deposit him behind the counter before locking the gate. He barks at Finn once and then discovers the bone he abandoned last night and launches himself at it. "She's the reason I called you, actually."

"Figured as much. Cormac said you were taking her case while he's in Florida." He picks an amethyst geode up from a shelf, hefting it in his hands. "What's up, brother? What do you need?"

"I need you to look into a couple of people for me. Her neighbor, Silas Wembley, and Thomas Huntington, who works for Ransom Oil. Both have been making nuisances of themselves."

"Ransom Oil." His expression hardens. "They're sniffing around?"

"They want her property," I confirm. "Her grandmother struck oil on it decades ago. I guess they caught wind of it and have been hounding her to sell. She's not interested."

"They've got a reputation." Finn sets the geode back on the shelf. "They were run out of Midland because of the way they went about buying up property from competitors. It cost them millions when it went to court."

"Did they get aggressive?"

"They got dirty," he says carefully. "Tried to compromise operations. One of their guys was convicted on racketeering charges."

"Jesus." I blow out a breath. "How long ago was this?"

"Ten, fifteen years ago?" Finn rubs his jaw. "It's been a hot minute. I only remember it because I did some work for the other company a few years back and came across some of the records when I was pillaging their system." He grins, his eyes dancing with humor. "I always get the good shit."

"I know. That's why I need you now." I grab a pen from the pen cup and use it to drag the letter across the counter for him to read. "This was waiting when we got here this morning. Don't touch it. Dillon needs to run it for prints."

He leans over the counter, his eyes scanning across the note. "Jesus Christ," he growls, his expression darkening. "Who the fuck leaves some shit like that for a woman?"

"That's exactly what I'd like to know. Dillon is doing what he can, but he's bound by the law. You aren't." I let that hang, knowing I don't need to say anything else. He knows exactly what I'm asking him to do. It's not the first time. Hell, I doubt it'll be the last time, either. Sometimes, the only way we can protect the people who need protecting is to navigate around the law.

Hacking isn't legal. But every law enforcement agency in the country would hesitate before hauling Finn in on charges. That's the kind of pull he has. I need that right now. Before the motherfucker terrorizing my woman has a chance to get close to her again.

"Give me a few days," Finn says without hesitation. "If there's anything to find, I'll find it."

"What was Finn doing here?" Dillon asks half an hour later, stomping into the shop like he owns the place.

"Shopping," I say, which is only partially a lie. He left here with a bag of stuff for his wife. "His wife likes the crystals in the window."

"You really think you can sell me that oceanfront property in Arizona, don't you?" Dillon cocks a brow at me, letting me know he isn't buying my bullshit. "What was he really doing here, Callum?"

"His wife likes the crystals in the window. If you hurry, I'm sure you can make it out there in time to check his receipt."

Dillon hits me with a hard look, the one they perfect in cop school. "We both know you're full of shit," he growls. "How about you tell me who you asked him to look into and save me the trouble of doing it myself?"

"Fuck" I curse. "You just can't leave shit alone, can you? He's looking into everyone on my fucking list—Silas, Huntington, and Ransom Oil." I shoot him a baleful glare. "You might want to do some digging on Ransom Oil while you're at it. They were run out of Midland, Texas fifteen years ago for pulling shit like this."

He grunts, reaching into his pocket to pull out a pair of gloves. "Let me see the note you found this morning."

I slide it across the counter toward him using the same pen from earlier.

"I assume you touched it?"

"So did Hope."

"Anyone else?"

"Nope."

He picks it up, scanning it. "Does she recognize the handwriting?"

"No."

"I'll get it to our fingerprint tech and see if he can pull anything from it." He pulls a bag from his pocket and flips it out before sliding the letter inside. "Find anything in the security footage?"

"Yeah." I queue up the footage of the note being delivered and play it for him. An hour before someone threw a rock through her window, a teenager in a dark hoodie walks into frame with his head down. He slips the note through the mail slot, then walks out of frame in almost the same place he entered.

A few seconds later, headlights beam across the front of the building and a small sliver of a small passenger car's fender and taillight can be seen. The car is a dark color, blue or black, maybe. But the taillight is busted.

It's not much to go on, but it's better than nothing. A teenager driving a small passenger car with a busted taillight is a starting point. He's a connection to whoever the fuck wrote that note.

"I'll get my guys on it." And then he frowns. "Where is Hope?"

"In the back." I sigh wearily. She's been hiding out there all morning. I had to go get her to ring Finn up. As soon as she was done, she fled back to the stockroom. I don't know what's going on in her head, but it's driving me fucking crazy. Every damn wall I knocked down yesterday feels like it's been rebuilt and buttressed since she found that damn note.

She's scared and trying like hell not to let me see it.

I can't miss it, though. Her fear burns like acid running through my veins. And there isn't a goddamn thing I can do about it beyond what I'm already doing. It doesn't feel like enough. Not even close.

"Find them, Dillon," I growl, not sure if it's a demand or a plea. "Whoever the fuck is behind this...I need you to help me find them."

He places a hand on my shoulder, squeezing. "We will, brother."

"Do you know what happened between her parents?" I ask after a moment, glancing up at him.

He jerks his chin in a nod. "Yeah, I'm familiar." His gaze runs across my face. "Why? You want to know what happened?"

"No. She'll tell me when she's ready to trust me with that part of her story. I just need to know... Did he hurt her too?" The question that's been eating at me ever since she told me what happened to her mom escapes in a painful rasp. "Did he... *Fuck*. Did he try to kill her too?"

"No," she whispers from behind us.

I spin around to find her standing in the doorway, her face pale. Her fathomless eyes wide.

"Firefly." I reach for her, but she evades me, stepping backward.

"He didn't hurt me."

"I should go," Dillon mutters. "I'll call if I find anything. Send me a copy of the security footage when you can. I'll try to track the kid down."

"Will do."

He beats a hasty retreat as Hope and I stare at each other in silence.

"I wasn't prying."

"We should go," she says at the same time.

"Go?" My brows pull down, confusion running through me. "Go where, Firefly?"

"Home." She wraps her arms around herself. "I completed the online orders, and the weather is keeping everyone inside today. I'll get more done in the shop at home than I will here."

"Are you sure?"

She nods.

I hesitate for a moment and then reluctantly give in. "Let's go home then, baby. We can talk when we get there."

Hope tries to evade me when we get home. As soon as I pull up behind her car, she's got Kieve in her arms, trying to climb from the truck.

I throw it in park, kill the engine, and hop out, circling around to cut her off on the sidewalk. Rain sheets down around us, drenching us both.

Kieve shivers in her arms, cold and miserable. She looks miserable too.

Poor little firefly.

"Come on. Inside with you," I murmur, scooping them both up into my arms to carry them the rest of the way to the door.

I set her on her feet on the porch, keeping my arms around her as she unlocks the door. Droplets of water roll down her chilled skin. Her shirt clings to her body. Even with her hair plastered to her head, she's the prettiest little firefly I've ever seen.

Kieve takes off for his pile of blankets beside the sofa as soon as we're over the threshold, burrowing in with loud complaints. No one ever accused him of suffering in silence.

I need to make sure they have umbrellas and raincoats next time.

Hope starts in his direction and then spins to face me. "He shot her because she was planning to take me and leave," she says, her voice shaking. "He'd gotten addicted to painkillers and was becoming volatile. Little things set him off. He locked me in my room one day while she was at work and wouldn't let me out. When she found out, she was furious. She didn't trust him with me anymore, so she was planning to leave. He found out."

"Jesus."

"You asked if he hurt me. He didn't in the way you meant it." She wraps her arms around herself, shivering. "But yeah, he hurt me, Callum. I went to school with two parents and came home with one in heaven and one bound for hell. I haven't spoken to him since that day."

I stride across the small foyer toward her, unable to keep my distance in the face of her pain. She allows me to pull her into my arms, though she stands stiffly.

"I stopped believing in fairytales and happily-ever-afters that day," she whispers against my throat. "I never wanted to believe again. But...then there was you."

I tip her chin up until her eyes meet mine. "What are you saying, Firefly?"

"You make me want to believe in forever, Callum." Her throat works, her eyes bottomless pools I could easily drown in and never even miss oxygen. "For the first time since I was ten, I believe in fairytales again."

"Jesus," I breathe, my voice shaking. I feather my fingers across her cheeks, staring at her in awe. She's so goddamn brave. I've known soldiers who have cracked under a tenth of the weight placed on her delicate shoulders, but not Hope. She carries her trauma, her fears, the crushing weight of what's happening to her, and every responsibility placed on her with her head held high. She doesn't bow beneath the weight. She doesn't break. She soldiers on.

"I need you."

"You have me, Firefly. You'll always have me." I press my mouth to hers, sealing my promise with a kiss. The heat between us grows, flames erupting to life as soon as she presses those sweet curves against me.

"Then make me yours, Callum," she whispers, commanding me to give her what she wants. "Make love to me."

Who the fuck am I to tell her no?

CHAPTER NINE

Hope

Callum sweeps me up into his arms, pressing his lips to mine as he carries me upstairs to my room. I shiver in his arms, but I'm not cold anymore. The chill left me as soon as he touched me. How can it withstand the flame of his touch? Nothing can. I melt into him, igniting all the way to my core. Nothing but want and need.

"Callum..." *I love you* is on the tip of my tongue, but the words stick in my throat, caught there by the fierce devotion in his eyes. It turns the pale emerald lush, like Ireland...the land that still beats in my blood. It beats in his too. I feel it in him, the magic. The fiery spirit. The unending capacity for good.

He's all those things.

Rain pelts the tin roof of the old farmhouse overhead as he carries me into the bedroom, each drop sounding like the discordant note of a long-forgotten song. It's captivating. Or maybe that's just the man wrapped around me, his rich scent intoxicating my senses.

"If it weren't storming, I'd put you in the shower," he murmurs, sliding me down his body until I land on my feet in front of him. He runs his hands down my arms as if to warm me. "Pamper you the way you deserve."

"You already do that."

A crooked grin dances at his lips as he brushes my tangled hair away from my face. "Get used to it, Firefly. I plan to do a lot of it."

"I've never had that before," I admit, though I'm guessing he already knows it. "I might be bad at it."

He chuckles, his breath pelting my lips. "Baby, I already know you're bad at letting yourself be cared for, but that's all right. You'll learn."

"Yeah? You're going to teach me?"

"Mmhmm." He bumps his nose against mine, reaching for the hem of my shirt. "Starting right now."

Even though he saw me practically naked yesterday and had his hands on intimate places today, I still squirm when he pulls my shirt off over my head before tossing it toward the bathroom. It lands on the floor with a wet plop.

His eyes flare with heat as he dips his head, settling his lips against the hollow of my collarbone.

I groan, digging my hands into his muscular upper arms to keep myself upright as he sucks right there, licking up raindrops from my skin.

"Delicious," he breathes, reaching for the clasp of my bra. He unhooks it with nimble fingers, peeling the lace fabric from my body.

As soon as it falls to the floor, I grasp the hem of his shirt, sliding it up his hard stomach. He helps me pull it off over his head, tossing it in the same direction mine went.

I run my hands down his bare chest, marveling at the way he trembles beneath my touch. He feels me just as acutely as I do him. He aches for me, just as much as I do for him.

We explore each other in silence as we strip, working together to shuck the wet jeans clinging to our legs. By the time we're naked, I'm a quivering mess.

"Beautiful," he growls, stepping back to look at me.

If I'm beautiful, he's transcendent, like an ancient Celtic warrior. His body is hewn from thick, corded muscle. His stomach isn't defined but one hard slab. The muscles in his arms and legs stand in testament to the sheer power of this man. And his erection....

I reach out, running my fingers down his thick shaft.

"Firefly," he groans, throwing his head back.

"You're so hard." I step closer, wrapping my hand around his length. Trying to, anyway. My fingers don't touch. I think that should probably intimidate me, but it doesn't. I want to know what it's like to have him inside me. Will it burn? Will it ache? Will he split me wide open? I want to find out.

A painful laugh rattles from his lips. "Believe me, baby, I'm aware. I've been that way since I met you. Ah, God. Squeeze just like that." He rocks his hips into my hand, writhing in ecstasy. His eyes are at half-mast, his gaze riveted to the sight of my hand on his cock. "Christ, I could come just watching you jack my cock, Firefly."

"Yeah?" I sink to my knees at his feet, putting myself at eye level with his erection. "And what if I do this, Callum?" I lean forward, flicking my tongue out to lick the broad head. His taste erupts on my tastebuds, salty and masculine. I groan and inch forward, wrapping my lips around him.

"Ah, goddamn, Firefly." He spears his hands into my hair, his fingers tugging at the tangles. "You're trying to kill me, aren't you?"

I moan around him.

"Watch your teeth, baby," he groans, instructing me on what to do. "Hollow your cheeks and suck when you plunge down. Fuck. Yeah, just like that." His hand tightens in my hair, his breath turning to a ragged pant. "Goddamn, you learn quick."

Pride roars through me at his praise. I press my legs together, the throb between them driving me crazy as I lick and suck, exploring him in a way that's new and exciting and far sexier than I ever imagined. He's completely at my mercy like this and yet...and yet somehow, he still manages to be the one in control as he thrusts between my lips.

I should hate it. I don't cede control or give it up to anyone. But with him, I don't want to be in control. I want to hand it over and let him lead. I trust him to take care of me. I fall backward into the loss of inhibition, reveling in the freedom it brings with it.

I plunge down again, taking him deeper. He hits the back of my throat, choking me. For just a moment, he holds me there. My throat closes around him. My eyes water.

"I feel you choking on my cock, Hope." He rocks his hips in tiny pulses. "I like it more than I should."

So do I. Oh, God. So do I.

Unable to resist, I slip a hand between my legs, touching myself, trying to relieve the ache there.

Callum roars, jerking backward. The next thing I know, I'm on my back on the bed with him on top of me, my legs spread wide around his hips as he glares down at me. "You touched my pussy."

"I...I..." I break off, writhing in torment.

"No one pleasures you but me, Hope," he growls, his eyes on fire. "No one touches what belongs to me. Not even you." He nips my throat, capturing my hands in one of his to pin them to the bed above my head. The other rakes down my abdomen before slipping between my thighs to part my folds. "When this perfect cunt aches, you come to me."

"Yes!" I agree as his thumb settles against my clit. "Yes, Callum."

He plays with me until I'm sobbing, his eyes locked on mine, claiming pieces of my soul. Possessing it. Or maybe it was his all along and he's merely taking ownership. I don't know. But he's in there, branding every dark corner with his name and his touch. And when I can't stand any more of his wicked torment, he pulls his hand away, kissing a hot trail down my body.

He rakes his teeth down my lower belly. Kisses my mound. His eyes glow as they meet mine. "Sing for me, Firefly," he breathes, lifting me toward his mouth.

I don't sing. I drown in his arms. His tongue spears through my folds, and I find heaven. It's right here in this bed with him. It's his mouth on me, his hands vises around my hips. His possessive growl ringing out around us.

He licks and sucks and bites, snarling as he eats me alive. The vibrations against my core add to the pleasure wracking my body, ratcheting it up a notch. He increases it a thousandfold when he works two fingers inside me, thrusting and stroking.

I sob and cry, babbling his name so loud it drowns out the storm outside. As my orgasm nears, I fight like hell to hold it off, not wanting this to end. But Callum knows what I'm doing. Somehow, he always sees me so clearly.

"Let go, Firefly," he demands, his voice a gritty rasp of sound. "You don't control what happens here. I do. You don't decide when you come or for how long, I do. Let go."

"Callum," I plead, begging him to let me stay just like this.

"Now, Firefly." His lips seam around my clit, sucking it into his mouth. His fingers curl up, stroking some magical spot inside.

I scream in defiance. I scream in ecstasy. I scream in submission. And I break, shattering into tiny pieces for him. Wave after wave batters me to the ground, unmaking me at the cellular level.

I emerge on the other side gasping for breath, trembling...stronger.

"Beautiful." Callum presses his lips to mine as he settles between my legs, notching his erection at my entrance. "My fierce little queen."

If I'm a queen, it's because he makes me feel like one.

"Are you ready to be mine?"

"I'm already yours, Callum."

"Yeah. You are." His smile lights up every corner of the room before he surges forward, pushing into me. His expression changes from joy to rapture as he slips inside, stretching me. He thrusts deep, sheathing himself inside.

I dig my nails into his shoulders, throwing my head back to cry his name into the room as he tears through my virgin barrier. There's pain. But there's beauty too. They're tied so tightly together, one fuses with the other, painting each stroke of his body into mine with ropes of each.

"Ah, Jesus, Firefly." His breath trembles at my lips, agony in his tone. "You're so fucking tight. Every time you breathe, you squeeze my cock like you're trying to brand him with your name."

"M-maybe I am." I drag my nails down his upper arms.

He presses his lips to my ear, nipping my lobe. "You don't have to brand him to claim him, sweet Hope. He already belongs to you. No one else will ever touch what belongs to you." He rolls us suddenly so I'm straddling his lap with my hands planted on his chest. "Now, ride me. I want to hear your ass clapping against my thighs every time you land."

Oh, sweet Jesus.

I lift up tentatively and then slide back down, trying to work out a rhythm. He helps guide me, using his hands on my hips to rock me against him. He's so much deeper this way, grinding against my cervix every time I drop down on him. The small bite of pain bleeds into pleasure, sending me reeling into another dimension.

I learn quickly. Within moments, I'm lifting up and dropping back down on him, riding him hard. He growls encouragements, his eyes at half-mast as he watches me in complete rapture.

"Such a fucking good girl." He bucks his hips to bounce me harder. "Look at you taking this dick like you were born to fuck."

"Callum." I claw at his thighs, his filthy mouth threatening to unravel me.

"I feel your cunt fluttering, Hope. You're going to come, aren't you?"

"Yes. God, yes," I cry, riding him hard. My ass lands against his thighs hard enough to sting as I slam myself down on him, chasing the pleasure looming like a wall directly ahead. I don't fight it this time. What's the point? He won't let me. As soon as I try, he'll punish me for it.

"Good."

I cry out as I go flying through the air, landing face down on the bed. Before my cry even ends, he's on me again, roughly shoving his way between my legs from behind. His body covers mine, pinning me to the bed as he thrusts into me hard.

"You're going to come just like this, Firefly," he breathes in my ear, yanking my hips up slightly so my ass is in the air and my upper body is prostrate on the bed. "I want you to feel me all the way in your fucking soul when I'm putting my kid in you."

I sob his name, clutching at the sheets as he pounds into me, one hand wrapped in my hair. The other runs down my body, touching me everywhere. He torments me as he fucks me, teasing me mercilessly. I writhe and sob, unable to move more than an inch or two because he's got me pinned in place.

It should frighten me. It should piss me off. But it doesn't. I love everything about his weight on top of me. I love having no control. I love being able to do nothing but take what he gives me. I love him. God, I love him so much it's terrifying and not nearly terrifying enough at the same time.

The orgasm slams into me like a tidal wave crashing into the shore. I topple beneath its might, shouting his name to the heavens. He roars mine back to me, falling still above me as his body jerks and wetness spills into me. No, not wetness. Him. His erection jerks as his seed splashes against my womb.

"Perfect," he groans in my ear, kissing all over the back of my neck as we writhe in ecstasy. "Fucking perfect, Firefly."

I'm not sure if he's talking about me or the moment. I'm not sure if it matters. In this moment, I think he's right on both counts. I feel perfect. And this is perfect. It's magic...the fairytale kind.

He falls beside me, dragging me into his arms with his cock still inside me. His chest heaves as he sucks in deep breaths, nuzzling his face into my throat from behind. "Never letting you go, sweet Hope. Never."

In this moment, I discover something else I lost too. *Hope.* The first fragile threads of it bloom in my heart, growing rapidly. Somehow, I'm going to make it through this. For him, I'll find a way.

"Get out!" I shout, marching toward the door of my shop when Thomas Huntington steps through the front doors late the next afternoon. "Out, out, out!"

"Miss Byrne." He holds his hands up in a placating gesture as Kieve starts barking up a storm from behind the counter. "I didn't come here to cause a problem. I just came to talk."

"I believe she made it clear when she threatened to shoot your sorry ass that she wasn't interested in what you had to say." Callum steps up beside me with his arms crossed over his chest. He angles his body so he's partially blocking me from view, protecting me with his body.

Thomas glances from me to Callum, his Good Ole' Boy smile on full display. It's a load of crap, of course. Thomas Huntington is nothing but a bully in a suit. He may hide it behind bright white veneers and Botox injections, but he's a thug.

If anyone is responsible for trying to destroy my business, it's him. I'd stake my life on it. He wants my land

and he'll do whatever it takes to get it for his company. Just like he does to every other property owner who has what he wants. There's a reason people sell to him. He hounds them into it. And when that doesn't work, he finds other ways to get what he wants.

Ransom Oil doesn't play fair. I doubt they even know the definition.

But they picked the wrong woman this time. There are no loopholes to exploit to get their dirty hands on my property. It's been in my family for generations, and Silver Spoon Falls protects its property owners specifically so companies like Ransom Oil can't come in and do what they do in every other town to run residents off. Sometimes, living in a town full of millionaires and billionaires pays off.

"Hello," Thomas says to Callum, thrusting out a hand toward him. "I'm Thomas Huntington with Ransom Oil."

"Callum Carmichael." Callum doesn't take his hand. "I know who you are. You've been harassing my woman about her property for months despite her telling you she isn't interested in selling."

"So you two have discussed it."

"You mean have we discussed the fact that you've continually trespassed on her property? Yeah, we've discussed it." Callum takes a threatening step toward him. "You won't listen to her. I guess she doesn't have the right appendage between her legs for a man like you to hear her, so listen up, Huntington. She said no. N-fucking-O. She isn't selling to you or anyone else." He pauses. "And just so we're clear, should anything happen to her, you still won't get your fucking hands on the property. Her will makes it crystal clear that the property will go to her cousin, Dante Arakas."

Thomas's smile slides from his face. "Dante Arakas is your cousin?"

"Yes," I lie, not sure what Callum is doing, but playing along anyway. "On my dad's side."

Thomas nods, his expression troubled. "Well, I guess if that's your decision," he sighs heavily, reaching into his pocket to pull out another of the business cards he's left me. "Here's my card if you change your mind, Miss Byrne."

"I won't."

Callum takes the card from him anyway, tucking it into his pocket.

We watch in silence as Thomas exits the shop.

"Dante Arakas is my cousin?" I arch a brow at him. "What are you up to now, Callum?"

"Protecting what belongs to me, Firefy." He tugs me into my arms. "If they are the ones behind the attacks, they're a helluva lot less likely to try to hurt you if they think they'll have to fight Dante Arakas if anything happens to you. You're one woman. He's the biggest criminal in Texas.

Who do you think they think they stand a better chance of talking down?"

I chew on my bottom lip, staring up at him. "What happens when he goes running to Dante to confirm your story?"

"I'll call Cormac." Callum shrugs. "Dante's niece is married to his MC brother. He'll float the story with Dante and make sure he's on board. Dante may be a criminal, but he's not a bad guy. Once he knows what's happening, he'll play along." He must read the skepticism on my face because he tips my chin up to place a kiss on my lips. "It'll be fine, Firefly. I don't need it to stick forever. Just long enough for Finn and Dillon to find something."

I exhale a breath, nodding.

CHAPTER TEN
Callum

"Are you fucking kidding me right now?" I growl, glaring balefully at the man standing on Hope's porch with his fingers hooked into the pockets of his blue jeans like he's some goddamn real cowboy.

It's been three days since Thomas Huntington showed up at Hope's store. Finn hasn't found anything yet. Neither has Dillon. But Cormac was able to get Dante Arakas on board with fucking over Ransom Oil if they come sniffing around him. Once he heard what was happening, he agreed to float that Hope is a cousin. I doubt Huntington has the balls to approach Dante, but on the off chance he does, our bases are covered.

As soon as we got home that night, Grizz and I spent half the night wiring up the property and installing cameras and motion lights. Imagine my goddamn surprise when Silas Wembley waltzed onto the front porch yesterday to filch the package that was delivered.

He beat a hasty retreat back to his place with it. Hope doesn't know yet and hasn't seen the footage. I don't intend to show it to her, but I changed the lock on her shop as soon as we got back from her store last night. I expected to find his ass waiting for her when we got home today, but I guess he was busy.

That's all right. He's here now. And Hope is occupied in the kitchen.

I yank the door open to glower at him. "Can I help you?"

"Oh." Silas seems taken aback by my presence, as if he didn't see my truck parked in the damn driveway. He quickly plasters a smile on his face, trying to hide the moment of surprise. "You're here again."

"Been here all week."

A split second of irritation flashes through his eyes before he schools his expression. "Is Hope busy? I have another package for her. I was going to leave it in the shop, but my key isn't working."

"Changed the locks." I step outside, pulling the door closed behind me before Kieve realizes he's here and tries to escape. Hope told me he doesn't care for Silas. As far as

I'm concerned, that tells me all I need to know about the man. "Changed the alarm code too."

"Ah. Well, if you'll just get Hope, I'll get the new information from her," he says, stepping back beside the package he left sitting on the porch.

"Yeah, that won't be happening." I lean against the door, shooting him a hard look. "Any packages left at your place can be delivered to the front door from now on. I'll make sure they get put where they need to be."

"I see." His false smile slides from his face. "Is Hope aware of this new arrangement?"

"She's the one who changed the alarm code."

"Well, then." He grits his teeth, though I think he intends to smile. "I suppose I'll get out of here and be about my business then."

"You do that," I say quietly.

He eyes me for a moment as if he wants to say something and then decides against it before turning to start down the steps.

"By the way," I say before he gets halfway down the sidewalk. "I installed cameras on the property the day before yesterday. Fascinating how much they pick up." I let that hang in the air for a minute before I continue. "Steal another package from her porch or show up here again making a nuisance of yourself, and you'll be explaining the footage to the sheriff."

"I was just trying to help her out."

"No, you weren't. You were trying to get in her fucking pants. She isn't interested. She'll never be interested. You watched her grow up, for fuck's sake. Stay away from her," I growl. "That's the only warning I'm going to give you."

He cowers like I just kicked him in the teeth. "Fine."

I stick around long enough to make sure he leaves and then scoop up the package and head inside. Hope may kick my ass when she finds out what I just did, but it had to be done. The fucker was stealing her mail just to bring it back to her. That's fucking weird no matter how you slice it.

I'm half convinced he isn't behind the attacks, though. I haven't entirely ruled him out yet, but part of me thinks maybe Hope is right and he's just a pervy old man with a crush. Christ. I hope that's all he is. Otherwise, I just kicked a hornet's nest.

"There you are," Hope says when I carry her package into the kitchen, depositing it on the counter. "Who was at the door?"

"Silas." I step up behind her at the stove, placing a kiss on the side of her throat as I wrap my arms around her from behind. "He dropped off your package."

"Oh." She shrinks in my arms. "Was he mad about the shop?"

"He stole the package from your porch yesterday, Firefly," I tell her quietly.

She spins to face me, shock written all over her face. "He didn't."

"He did. I caught it on camera."

Her face falls and then she groans, faceplanting into my chest. "I want to say I'm surprised, but nothing surprises me anymore. He's always been odd." She lifts her head to look at me. "I still don't think he's the one trying to hurt me though, Callum. I think he's just Silas." She scrunches up her face. "Is it weird that I'm relieved the carrier isn't delivering my packages to the wrong place?"

"Nah, Firefly. The only thing weird here is your fucking pervert neighbor."

"Callum."

"He watched you grow up, he's nearly forty years older than you, and he's basically stalking you. It's fucking weird, Firefly. I'm just calling it like I see it," I murmur, tucking her hair behind her ears.

"It is weird," she mumbles.

"He won't be a problem anymore."

"You threatened him, didn't you?"

"I simply reminded him that mail theft is a crime and I have footage."

"So you threatened him."

"Pretty much." I shrug, unrepentant. I never promised to fight fair. I promised to keep her safe. I'll do whatever I have to do to protect her, even if it means holding that footage over that fucker's head until the day he dies.

She shakes her head, laughing quietly.

I press my lips to her forehead and then shuffle her to the side. "Go sit down and let me finish dinner, baby. Then I'm going to take you upstairs and have you for dessert."

"Maybe I'll have you for dessert, Callum Carmichael," she retorts, her hands on her wide hips and fire in her eyes.

"Well, shit. In that case, maybe we'll skip dinner."

"More," Hope moans, writhing against the shower wall as I pound into her, running my finger in circles around her clit at the same time. "Oh, God, Callum. More."

I roar her name and give her everything I have, fucking her so hard my balls slap against her slippery skin with a resounding smack on every thrust. She claws down my back, shouting my name with her head thrown back against the shower wall.

"Come, Firefly. Christ. I need you to fucking come." I bend my head forward, closing my teeth around one hard nipple.

She shouts my name, exploding around me.

I practically sob in relief as my balls give up the fight and I follow her over the edge, locking my legs to keep from collapsing in a heap on the floor of the shower. She feels too fucking good when she's wrapped around me, dripping all over my balls, squeezing my cock in a vise.

I can't stay out of her. I fucked her after dinner last night, and again before we went to sleep. As soon as she climbed into the shower with me, I was on her again, pressing her back against the wall. She's got my dick in a permanent state of arousal. Every move she makes has me ready to go, aching like a motherfucker to feel her wrapped around me again.

I stopped falling for her days ago. I landed face-first into love. I keep waiting for the perfect moment to tell her, hoping the sword hanging over her head will disappear soon. But I'm fucking tired of waiting. Every moment with her is perfect. I'm more alive with her than I've ever been. Today is St. Patrick's Day. If any day is fitting to tell her she has my heart, it's this one. If any moment is perfect, it's this one. When she's wrapped around me, purring like a little kitten.

"*Tá mo chroí istigh ionat*," I whisper in her ear, the same thing my dad always tells my mom. *My heart is in you.* I nuzzle my face against her throat, listening to her little gasp of delight. "I love you, Firefly."

"Callum," she breathes, her voice trembling. "I love you too."

Jesus. My eyes fall closed, her sweet words washing over me in a warm flood. They wash through me, sending a flurry of soft emotion soaring high. Peace. Hope. Joy. Reverence. Love. So much of it, I can't breathe through it.

I lift my head, pressing my lips to hers in a soft kiss. We stay just like that for a long moment, lost in each other and the moment. At least until the hot water turns ice cold. It doesn't happen little by little. It happens all at once.

"Jesus Christ," I growl, rushing to turn the knobs off as she shrieks and tries to avoid the bone-chilling spray. "We're replacing the water heater, Firefly. This one doesn't last long enough."

"We've been in here for an hour, Callum."

"Exactly. That's not long enough." I drag her out of the shower, plucking a towel from the rack to wrap around her as she shivers, her eyes bright with happiness. "I need at least two hours of hot water to properly appreciate you naked and soapy."

She rolls her eyes at me, quickly rubbing the towel over herself to sop up the water. I stand with mine in my hands, enjoying the show. What? She's fucking naked and she's beautiful. I'm not *that* cold.

"Your phone is ringing."

"What?"

"Your phone is ringing," she says again, smirking at me as she wraps the towel around her, hiding her gorgeous body from view. It's a travesty, really.

"Shit." I quickly dry off and then jog toward the bedroom to grab it from the nightstand where I left it. Dillon's name flashes across the display, along with a slew of missed calls. *Fuck.* Something's wrong.

I swipe to answer, striding out of the bedroom to keep Hope from hearing whatever bad news he's about to deliver.

"What's up?"

"I need you and Hope to get down to Hope's shop," he says without preamble. "We have a situation."

"What kind of situation?"

"We found the van that tried to drive her off the road."

"Who was driving it?"

"We don't know."

"What do you mean you don't know?" I growl, pacing the hall. "Did you run the fucking tags? Who is it registered to?"

"It's a stolen vehicle, Callum." He mutters a curse under his breath. "Someone put a brick on the gas pedal and drove it through the front of her shop before dawn this morning. It's currently sitting in the middle of her store."

"Fuck."

"We need her down here." He pauses. "You need to prepare her, man. I don't know how much everything in the shop cost, but she's looking at thousands of dollars worth of damage to the building alone."

I close my eyes, rage and defeat coursing through me in tandem. This is going to break her fucking heart. No. *I'm* going to break her fucking heart because I'm the one who has to deliver the news. I'm going to find whoever did this and kill them slowly.

"We'll be there within the hour," I tell Dillon before hanging up on him. I stand in the hallway for a minute, trying to get my emotions under control before I walk back in there and tell Hope that everything she's worked so hard for is gone.

The worst goddamn part about it is that I still don't know who to blame. Silas Wembley? Thomas Huntington? Either is just as likely as the other. Both have motive. Both are shady as shit. I've pissed in both of their Cheerios this week.

Christ. Is that why her store was destroyed? Because I poked the bear?

The thought is sobering. I'm supposed to protect her, but I'm failing her. At every goddamn turn, I'm failing her.

"Callum?" She pokes her head out into the hallway. "Is everything okay?"

I take a breath and turn to face her. "Come here, Firefly."

The smile slides from her face. The brightness dims in her eyes. She fades right in front of me, shrinking before my eyes. "What happened?" she whispers, pacing slowly toward me. "Just tell me."

I pull her into my arms, wrapping them tightly around her. There's no real way to soften the blow. She wouldn't want me to even if I could, so I tell her plainly. "Early this morning, someone drove a van through the front of your store, Firefly. Dillon is waiting for us down there now."

She flinches in my arms, the lights winking out in her eyes. Just like that, whoever is behind this accomplishes what they've been trying to do all along. They break her.

And for that alone, I'm going to kill them.

CHAPTER ELEVEN
Hope

I walk through the destruction of my store with my arms wrapped around myself, completely numb. A construction crew installed support beams so the wrecker service could remove the truck an hour ago. Dillon reluctantly agreed to let me inside to look around. I wish I hadn't insisted. The store is in shambles. My dreams lie in shattered, twisted ruin. Somewhere among the wreckage are centuries of remedies passed down through generations.

I'm not a healer like my granny was. I don't have a green thumb like my grandpa did. All I have is the knowledge they left me and the love I poured into this place. I can't replace most of what was here. The plants stopped growing when Granny got too sick to tend to them.

It's funny. Whoever wants my land ensured the only thing I had left was the land. They took everything else when they sent that van careening through the front of my store.

I choke on a sob, trying hard to fight it back.

"Firefly." Callum reaches for me, but I take a step back. If he touches me right now, I'm going to fall apart. I can't do that here with dozens of people looking on. When I crack, I want it to be in the privacy of our home, in the shelter of his arms. Not here with half the sheriff's office and the fire department looking on.

"I want to go home," I mumble.

"The insurance adjuster is on the way, baby."

"I don't care. I just want to go home."

"I can drop her off before I meet Finn to do that thing we discussed earlier," Cormac offers, stepping up beside his cousin. He's a giant, standing head and shoulders taller than everyone except Callum. He's usually loud and boisterous, but he's subdued now. "You can wait for the insurance guy."

Callum looks torn.

"I'll be fine. We have cameras now." I try to smile at him, but it wobbles on my face. "I'll keep Kieve close and lock the door until you get home."

"Fuck." He pulls me into his arms to kiss me hard on the mouth. "Fine. But you keep the doors locked, Firefly. I'll be there as soon as the insurance adjuster is done here."

"Okay." I press my forehead to his for a brief moment and then pull away.

"I love you."

"I love you too."

Cormac leads me out of the wreckage of my store toward a massive truck pulled up beside Callum's. He has to help me climb in. Even with the step on the side, my legs are too short. I have a feeling he probably has it that way just so he has to help his wife get in when they take his truck.

We have to navigate around fire trucks and police cruisers to get out of the parking lot. The entire parking lot is still cordoned off as a crime scene. God. My store is now a crime scene.

"You'll rebuild, Hope," Cormac rumbles, letting me know I said that out loud. "We won't let you fail. That's not how it works here. We take care of our own."

"There's nothing left to rebuild." I glance out of the window to hide the tears in my eyes. "I can't mix the salves and ointments that require plants and flowers that were destroyed. Most of my stock was in that store."

"Shit."

"Yeah."

We drive in silence until we're nearly to my house and then Cormac speaks up again. "You know Callum was in the Army?"

"He told me. Special Forces."

"Yeah. When my girl was in danger, he's the person I trusted to guard her back because he doesn't fail. The word isn't in his vocabulary. When it counts, he comes through, no matter what." He glances over at me as he pulls into my driveway. "It counts more than ever this time because you matter more than anything ever has to him. Don't give up yet, sweetheart. He won't fail you, and he won't let you fail."

"Thank you," I whisper, my throat tight. "For everything, Cormac."

He grins at me, flashing his dimples. "Anytime. You're family. We always protect our family." He jerks his chin toward the house. "Go on inside and lock the doors. I'll wait until you're inside."

I nod and open the door, wiggling down from his truck. I head straight for the door, waving once I get it unlocked. Cormac waves back but doesn't move an inch until the front door closes behind me.

Kieve lifts his head from his pile of blankets to glare at me.

As soon as I hear Cormac's truck backing down the driveway, I slide down the door, wrap my arms around myself, and give into the tears I've been holding at bay all morning. They come in gasping sobs, wracking my body.

Kieve whines and then I hear his tiny nails tapping against the floor as he runs toward me. He squeezes his way onto my lap, stretching his neck up to lick my face.

"Oh, Kieve," I whisper, holding him. "What are we going to do?"

He whines softly as if to say he doesn't know.

That makes two of us.

I'm still sitting in the same spot when Callum pulls into the driveway an hour later. I carefully set Kieve on his feet and wipe my face, though I know there's no hiding the fact that I've been crying. Callum will see right through me. He always does.

From the very beginning, he's seen me more clearly than anyone else ever has. He knows me in ways no one ever has. I didn't need Cormac to tell me that Callum won't fail me. I know he won't. He'll find whoever destroyed my store. He'll make sure they pay. But it won't bring back what they took.

There is no breathing life back into the garden that died long before my granny did...the one my grandpa tended so carefully. All those flowers and herbs are gone. My mom helped him tend so many of those flowers. And now, one of my last connections to her is gone. It hurts a little bit like losing her all over again.

I carefully climb to my feet and unlock the door before stepping out onto the porch to greet Callum. Except when I lift my head, it's not Callum's truck parked in the driveway. And it's not Callum striding up the sidewalk toward me.

Thomas Huntington.

I take a quick step back toward the house, hoping to make it back inside before he sees me. It's St. Patrick's Day. Luck should be on my side at least once today. But it isn't.

"Miss Byrne." His hazel eyes meet mine, a grim smile on his face.

"I thought we agreed you weren't going to show up on my property anymore, Mr. Huntington," I say, proud when my voice doesn't shake. "You need to leave."

"I'm afraid I can't do that. We need to talk."

"We have nothing to talk about."

"I know what happened to your store."

I hesitate, not sure if he means he heard what happened or if he means he knows what happened because he's responsible. "Everyone in town knows what happened," I mutter. "I'm sure it's the talk of the town."

"You know that isn't what I mean."

"Then what do you mean? Did you destroy my store?" I growl.

"I had nothing to do with that," he says, holding up his hands. "I won't stand here and say that I'm innocent in any of the misfortunes that have befallen you lately. I regret that I was...deceived."

"Deceived?" I gape at him. God, he even talks like a good ole' boy, dancing around the point, trying to tidy it up in pretty language like that'll change the fact that he and his company have been trying to kill me. "You and your company have been trying to kill me to get my land!"

"I was trying to scare you, not hurt you, Miss Byrne. Had I known about your connection to Dante Arakas, I can assure you, I never would have gotten involved in this scheme." He expels a breath. "I'm trying to make it right now."

No, he isn't. He's trying to absolve himself of guilt because he thinks Dante Arakas is my cousin.

"How can you possibly make this right?" I cry. "You and your company destroyed my store. You destroyed the only connection I had left to my grandfather and my mom." My voice cracks. "How could you *possibly* make that right?"

"You misunderstand," he says softly. "Ransom Oil had nothing to do with what happened to your store, Miss Byrne."

"What? What are you saying? You just told me that you guys are the ones behind everything!"

"I haven't been working alone."

I gape at him, shocked silent. And then my stomach begins to churn as suspicion grows, sending bile crawling up my throat. He isn't working alone. Of course he isn't. "Who?"

"Your neighbor, Silas Wembley."

I knew he was going to say that, but hearing it sends all the air rushing out of my lungs anyway. Silas is behind this? God, I should have listened to Callum on day one. He was right all along. My neighbor isn't just a creep. He's a psycho.

"Why?" I ask, completely numb.

"He wanted you and the money. We wanted the land." Mr. Huntington has the grace to look apologetic. "He thought if we teamed up, we could both get what we wanted. He failed to disclose that you're related to Arakas."

"Who tried to drive me over the edge of The Falls?"

"Silas."

A small movement in my peripheral catches my attention. I glance toward the back of Mr. Huntington's silver truck just in time to see Silas step out from behind it, a pistol in his hands and a sneer on his face.

"I should have known I couldn't trust you," he growls at Thomas Huntington, aiming the gun at him. He doesn't even flinch as he pulls the trigger.

I scream, jumping backward.

Mr. Huntington stumbles forward a step as a pool of red blooms across his chest. He lists to the side, his expression contorting. And then he falls.

Silas steps over him without a second glance, training the gun on me. "Hi, sweetheart," he says as if he didn't just shoot someone in cold blood. As if he didn't destroy my business and my life this morning. As if he has any right to call me that. "It didn't have to end this way, you know."

"You're insane," I whisper, the first words that come to mind. They're true. He is insane. How else was it supposed to end? What fantasy did he concoct in his mind? I'd run into his arms in search of safety, and we'd live happily ever after on the money Ransom Oil paid for the land? My stomach churns at the thought. *God*. That probably is what he thought would happen.

Except Silas Wembley isn't hero material. When I needed protection, he was the last person I thought about. He's the man I grew up next door to, nothing more. That's all he's ever been to me. It's all he ever would have been to me. Now, he's a monster.

"I never would have given myself to you," I snarl. "Never."

He laughs in my face, climbing the stairs toward me. "You think this was about you, Hope? Taking you to my bed would have been a nice bonus, but you were never the prize. You were just a means to an end. The money was the prize." He stops in front of me, his boots touching the toes of my ballet flats. "One million dollars. Only an idiot walks away from cash like that."

"Then I guess I'm an idiot."

"You said it, not me."

"Some things are more important, Silas. This land has been in my family for generations. It's the only connection I have left to my family. Money can't replace any of that."

"And loyalty to bones rotting in the ground can't keep you fed and warm," he snaps. "Get inside, Hope."

"Why? So you can shoot me in the living room? No, thanks."

"I'm not going to shoot you. You're going to clear the security footage," he says. "And then you're going to tell the world that Thomas Huntington showed up here, threatening to kill you. You'll tell the world that he admitted to everything. And then you're going to sell the land to me."

"If I don't?"

"Then I kill your boyfriend." He smiles at me, the same damning, pleasant smile he always wears. It's so patently false, I don't know how I never saw it before now. "And then you. The choice is yours."

CHAPTER TWELVE
Callum

"Callum."

I glance up from the paperwork the insurance adjuster left for Hope to see Finn striding across the parking lot toward me, a deep furrow between his brows and his lips pursed. He looks worried. The fact that he's not with Cormac worries me. He was supposed to go with him to have a not-so-polite chat with Huntington.

Fuck.

I toss the paperwork into the passenger side of my truck and jog across the parking lot toward him, meeting him halfway. "What's up?"

"I found something," he says.

"What?"

"You aren't going to like it."

"Tell me."

"Silas Wembley and Thomas Huntington have been in contact." He pulls his phone out of his pocket, glancing over his shoulder to make sure we're alone. "I shouldn't have this, but I hacked into Wembley's phone records. He's been talking to Huntington two or three times a week for the last two and a half months."

"Jesus Christ," I breathe, my stomach sinking to my feet. "The motherfuckers are working together." Why didn't I see it before? I know why. Because I wanted it to be Silas so goddamn badly it never crossed my mind that it could be both of them.

"There's more," Finn warns me. He pulls up an email chain on his phone, dated yesterday.

To: cbeeson@ransomoil.org
From: thuntington@ransomoil.org
Subject: Silver Spoon Falls Property

I've advised our partner that we're no longer interested in the property. Expect trouble. Should I warn the girl?

-T

To: thuntington@ransomoil.org
From: cbeeson@ransomoil.org
Re: Silver Spoon Falls Property

Yes. Minimize blowback. You know what to do.

-Charles

"Looks like they let Silas know they were pulling out of whatever deal they made with him," Finn says. "I'm guessing because they think Arakas is her cousin. And it sounds like they were intending to warn her about him to take the heat off of them."

"That's what it sounds like to me too." I drag my phone from my pocket, fury pumping through my system as I dial Cormac's number.

"Yo."

"I need you to get back to Hope's," I growl. "Silas Wembley is our guy. If I find him, I'm killing him."

"Shit, brother. If you're asking me to stop you, you called the wrong motherfucker today. I might just help." Cormac blows out a breath. "I just checked Huntington's room. He's not here. I'll head back to Hope's."

"Meet you there."

I disconnect and dial Dillon. He's around here somewhere, but I don't have time to chase his ass down. I need to get to my girl now. She's out there alone, and Silas is right next door.

"Are you heading out?" Dillon asks as soon as he answers.

"Silas Wembley was working with Thomas Huntington. Finn found phone records. He also found emails from Thomas Huntington to someone at Ransom about pulling out of their deal with Silas. They were going to warn Hope. Finn and I are heading to her place now. Cormac is meeting us there."

"Shit," Dillon growls. "I'm on my way."

"You better beat me there, Dillon," I say quietly. "If I find him before you do, I'll kill him. I don't give a fuck if you're the sheriff. You won't be able to stop me."

"Who the fuck says I'd try?" He hangs up on me.

"Let's roll."

"I'll drive."

I toss Finn my keys without complaint, knowing he's in a better frame of mind to get us there than I am. I'm as liable to run us into a ditch than I am to get us to Hope in one piece.

I dial her number.

Pick up, Firefly. Please, pick up.

Dillon whips into the driveway two seconds ahead of Finn who drives my truck like he fucking stole it. I'm surprised the damn tires aren't smoking when we pull up. My hackles rise as soon as I see the silver truck in the driveway.

And then my gaze lands on Thomas Huntington's body sprawled across the sidewalk. My blood runs cold. I'm out of the truck and sprinting for the door before Finn even has it in park.

Dillon grabs me, tackling me to the ground halfway to the house.

I roar, trying to throw him off me.

"Callum, goddammit!"

Footsteps race toward us before Finn drops to his knees, helping Dillon pin me in place. I fight against both of them, trying like hell to break free to get to Hope. If he hurt her. Ah, Christ. If he hurt her...

"Think for a minute, goddammit," Dillon barks. "If he's got her in the house and you go rushing in there, you're putting her life at risk. And if she's..."

"Don't you fucking say it," I snarl. "Don't say it."

"Easy, brother," Finn says. "Easy."

She's alive. She has to be alive. I'd know if she weren't. Half of my soul would be gone. And it's not. It's still blazing bright as the sun, pulsing like a second, vital heartbeat inside me. He's inside with her right now, doing God only knows what.

Ah, God, Firefly. I'm sorry. I'm so fucking sorry I wasn't here.

"We have to go in. He has her in there, goddammit." I push against their hold again, meeting their gazes. "If she were your wives, you'd go in. You know you would."

Dillon curses.

Finn releases me, holding his hands up.

"You aren't going in without a fucking gun," Dillon snaps, reluctantly letting me go.

I climb to my feet, everything in me screaming for me to make a run for the door. But he's right. If I'm going in, the only way that bastard is coming out is in a body bag. That's the only way this ends. It's inevitable at this point. It was from the moment he hurt her the first time.

I'm not tame. I'm not civilized. When it comes to her, I'm willing to do whatever it takes to make her mine and keep her safe. He touched what didn't belong to him. He hurt her. He has to pay for that. I won't fucking rest until he does.

I stomp back to my truck, popping the glove compartment to retrieve my gun.

Dillon sighs in exasperation when he sees it. "Of course you have a goddamn gun in the glove compartment."

"This is Texas," Finn mutters. "Everyone has a gun in the glove compartment."

Cormac pulls into the driveway before Dillon can say anything else. He throws it into park and climbs out with the engine still running, jogging toward us. He spares a quick glance at the body on the ground, quickly assessing the situation, and then his eyes come to me. "What's the play?"

"We're going in."

"Fucking right we are."

"I've got backup on the way."

Cormac shoots Dillon a wicked grin. "Won't need it. He'll be handled before they get here. Who's got the front and who gets the back?"

"I'll take the back with Dillon since I'm not armed," Finn says. "You and Callum can have the front. Let's do this shit."

Cormac heads for the front door without hesitation, ready to throw down. His big ass is always ready. I'm right beside him, ready to get to my girl. Dillon mutters a curse and then he and Finn head toward the back of the house.

"You better find him quick," Cormac mutters. "We've got about a sixty second head start on Dillon. After that, all bets are off."

We pound up the front steps together, not bothering to be quiet about it. There's no hiding the fact that we're here. If he's in there with Hope, he already knows we're coming in after him.

Don't let him win, Firefly. Whatever you do, don't let him win. I'm coming for you. I promise.

I try the door, surprised when it opens. The fucker didn't even bother locking it. Either he's cocky, he's stupid, or they aren't here. A bullet slams into the wooden frame, splintering wood right beside my face.

So he's stupid, then. Got it.

"Shit," Cormac growls.

Hope shouts my name as another gunshot rings out. Kieve barks his little head off and then yelps. Oh, that motherfucker better not have hurt him.

I kick the door open, trying to get a visual on what's happening inside. My blood boils when I see Hope running across the foyer with tears streaming down her face. Silas is a few feet behind her, trying to shake Kieve off where the dog has latched onto his hand.

Cormac and I burst through the door at the same time.

"Callum!" Hope sobs.

"Run, baby. Go."

She sobs again, but obeys, stumbling past me out of the house.

Silas grabs Kieve by the collar, flinging him across the room. He lands on the couch, yelping. I don't think he's hurt though. I think he's just offended. Blood drips from small wounds on Silas's hand as he fumbles for the gun he dropped.

I don't give him time to get his hands on it.

"You piece of shit," I roar, cracking him over the back of the head with the butt of my gun. I toss the gun aside and land a blow against his right cheek, and then another to his nose. Cartilage crunches beneath my fist as it breaks. I hit him again, and then again, and then one final time before I let his sorry ass fall to the floor.

"You're lucky you're in her home or you'd be dead right now, you sorry motherfucker," I growl, dragging him up by the collar of the shirt to look him in the eye. "That's the only reason you're still breathing right now. You come near her ever again, I'll bury you so deep no one will ever find your body."

I toss him back to the ground, stepping away from him.

"Good man," Cormac says, clamping a hand on my shoulder as Dillon and Finn step forward to haul Silas to his feet. I never even heard them come in. Dillon didn't even try to stop me from beating the hell out of him. Guess he knew the fucker had it coming. "Go take care of your girl. We've got this little bitch."

"Kieve, *tar anseo.*"

He inches toward me, hesitant to approach.

I squat, holding out my hand for him. "Come here, boy. I won't hurt you."

He whines and then darts forward allowing me to pick him up.

I carry him outside with me.

"Callum!" Hope sobs, rushing toward us.

I wrap one arm around her, dragging her up against my chest and holding on tight as Kieve jumps up to lick her face. She's safe. Thank fucking God. She's finally safe.

CHAPTER THIRTEEN

Hope

Two Weeks Later

"I love you." Callum reaches across the console for my hand, bringing my fingers up to his lips to press a kiss to them.

"I love you too."

"It'll be okay," he promises.

I smile at him bravely. We're going back to the store for the first time since Silas destroyed it. I haven't had the heart to go back since. After he killed Thomas Huntington and tried to force me to sell the land to him, Callum hired someone to board up the store and took me away for a few days. We just left everything behind and went to Nashville for a week with Kieve.

I needed the change of scenery. I needed time and distance to process and deal with everything that happened. Spending time with his family helped. His parents are amazing. Meeting his mom was bittersweet. It reminded me of everything I've missed with my mom but made me appreciate the time I did have with her.

It also reminded me that the last of the plants may be gone, but my biggest connection to her will always be my memories. Those aren't in the plants she grew with my grandfather. They aren't in the house she grew up in. They aren't in the land she played on as a little girl. Those I carry with me everywhere. So long as I carry her in my heart, she'll live on.

I needed that reminder. I think I've needed it for a long time.

I'm looking forward to making new memories with Callum's mom. I already love her. She's so sweet. She'll never replace my mom. She wouldn't even dream of trying, but it's nice to have a warm, motherly hug and a loving ear again. I've missed that so much since my mom and then Granny died.

We got back into town a few days ago, but I've been avoiding going to the store. Not because I wasn't ready to face it again, but because cleaning it up is going to be a nightmare. I don't like cleaning on a good day. The store looks exactly like someone drove a vehicle through it. It's going to take forever to sort through everything and take stock of what is salvageable and what isn't.

But I'm ready to do it. Silas doesn't get to win. He doesn't get to take a single damn thing from me. Not my dreams, not my store, not hope. Nothing. I refuse to allow him to do it. He's a monster, and monsters don't win in the end. They die miserable, exactly like they were always supposed to. That's what's in store for him.

He's facing life in prison for murder, and then about fifteen additional felony charges including kidnapping, burglary, three counts of attempted murder for trying to run me off the road and then trying to shoot Cormac and Callum, and various other crimes. Dillon even made sure he was charged with stealing my mail. It's a small thing given everything else he's facing but seeing that charge on the list made Callum's whole day. It made mine too.

Silas Wembley won't ever get out again. I had the option of pressing charges against Ransom Oil but decided not to do it. In the end, they did the right thing even if they did it for the wrong reasons. And their misdeeds cost the life of one of their employees. The world knows what they did. Their stock has plummeted.

We served them with cease-and-desist paperwork and formally trespassed all representatives for the company from any of my property. It's a formality at this point since they'll likely be out of business by the end of the year, but Callum didn't want to take any chances.

To be honest, neither did I. I'll sleep better at night knowing they'll face criminal charges if they come near me or my property.

"What in the world?" I stare out the window at the packed parking lot in front of my store, trying to process why so many people are crammed into the small lot. Is the coffee shop having a fire sale or something? And then I see the front of my store. "Callum," I whisper, my voice shaking. "What...?"

"People in town have been working all week, Firefly. Everyone pitched in. What insurance didn't cover, they donated. I'm still working on replacing some of the plants and flowers that were destroyed, but they're being shipped in from all over the world for you." He pulls into an empty spot near the front of the lot, turning to face me. "I know they won't replace the memories the ones you lost held, but they'll keep you in business."

"Callum." Tears well in my eyes as I gape between him and the townspeople repainting the front of the store. It's as if Silas never destroyed it. Every last trace of the destruction he left behind is gone, replaced by the people who live here. "You did all of this for me?"

"Didn't I tell you, Firefly? There isn't a single fucking thing on this earth I wouldn't do for you." He unlatches my seatbelt, pulling me across the console onto his lap. "You're my world, sweet Hope. Taking care of you is what I was put here to do." He tips my chin up, placing a soft kiss on my lips. "And I didn't do it alone. Everyone out there right now helped. Because you forgot something important about that water you sell."

"What did I forget?"

"It makes people fall in love," he whispers. "And everyone in this town has fallen in love with you just as hard as I did, Firefly. You aren't alone anymore."

I bury my face in his shoulder, sobbing.

"No crying, sweet Hope." He brushes his lips against my ear. "You still have to agree to be my wife and then go out there and thank everyone. We both know how much you hate to cry in public."

I lift my head on a gasp to find him grinning at me, my favorite crooked grin.

"Yeah, you heard me," he says, chuckling as he reaches into his pocket. "Marry me, Firefly. And before you answer, just know that you aren't allowed to say no. It's not an option."

"Says who?"

"Me." He pulls a ring out of his pocket, holding it out to me in the palm of his hand. Intricate Celtic knots surround the massive solitaire diamond on the platinum band. It's a beautiful ring. Way too fancy for a woman like me, but I'm not holding that against him. I'm not telling him no, either.

"Well, in that case," I say, sniffling. "I guess I'll let you know later."

He growls, grabbing my hand to slip the ring onto my finger. "The answer is yes, Firefly. You're marrying me."

"Okay," I agree, wrapping my arms around his neck to pull him down for a kiss. "I guess since you're being bossy about it, I'll give you what you want."

"See? Now you're learning." His lips touch mine, setting my soul on fire all over again.

EPILOGUE
Callum

Five Years Later

"I told you to be quiet, Firefly," I growl, biting Hope's lip when she moans my name a little too loud. "If the kids hear you, I'll have to stop what I'm doing to you."

"Don't you dare stop." She glares at me, dragging her nails down my back. "I will murder you, Callum."

"Then cover your mouth like a good girl and bounce on my cock like I fucking told you." I lift her up and drop her down, biting my tongue to keep from shouting her name into the dark. Fuck. She feels too good.

How is it possible that she gets even tighter every time I'm in her? It's a mystery I've been trying to solve for five years, and I still don't have an answer. She still drives me out of my mind every time I get inside her. And let's be honest, I'm inside her at every available opportunity. Even if I have to drag her into the dark laundry room while the kids watch a movie in the living room.

I'm shameless when it comes to her, and nothing stands in my way. I won't allow it to. This woman is my world. She's the reason I breathe. Hell, sometimes I think she may be the air I breathe. Every single piece of me belongs to her.

She feels the same way about me. I see it in her eyes every time she looks at me. And fuck if that doesn't make me feel like a goddamn king. If the water in this town is magic, I got the keeper of it when I found her.

Five years later, she's still magic to me. And she still brings magic to people who need it. Her store is thriving. Silver Spoon Falls water is in every grocery store in town and several others throughout the county. She still offers it in small quantities online, alongside the herbal remedies her grandmother taught her. She has a full-time employee at the store now, and two at the shop here. She's happier than she's ever been, and so am I.

"Callum," she moans again, louder than she should. There's no keeping her quiet. When she's on my cock, she's loud no matter what. "Oh, God. Oh, God."

I drag her up and down my cock, trying to get her there before three curious little boys come bursting in to see why mommy is praying in the laundry room again. At this point, they're convinced she's Mother Teresa because I've got her praying all over the house.

Like I said, I'm shameless. I'm not sorry about it, either.

I press her back against the wall, allowing me to tilt her hips higher. I pound into her, angling my hips to hit her g-spot with every thrust. My lips cover hers, my tongue tangling with hers to muffle her cries.

She comes hard, soaking my cock with her juices.

I groan into her mouth and follow her over the edge, writhing in ecstasy.

"Daddy! Keegan stole my popcorn!" Our four-year-old, Nolan shouts.

"Did not!" His three-year-old brother, Keegan yells back.

"Did too! I sawed you!"

I bury my face in Hope's throat, chuckling. "Well, at least they let us finish this time." I reluctantly slide out of her, groaning as soon as my dick slips free. I fucking hate losing her heat. I push my cum back inside her and then fix her panties before helping her step back into her shorts.

Once she's put back together, I tuck my cock back inside my pants.

"Give it back right now, Keegan!" Nolan screeches.

"Good grief. What are they doing out there?"

"Judging by the sounds of it, they haven't killed each other yet." I tug her back into my arms when she turns toward the door to go check on the boys. Screaming is normal around here. It's the silence that's dangerous. When they're shouting, I know it's business as usual. But when they get quiet? That's when they're up to some bullshit. It never fucking fails.

They usually drag Aiden along for whatever trouble they're causing. He's barely two, but he follows Nolan and Keegan around, picking up every troublemaking habit they teach him. They're exactly like their uncle and I were when we were kids.

I love the hell out of them.

I splay my hand across Hope's belly, nuzzling my nose against hers. "If you give me another son this time, I'm spanking your gorgeous ass, Firefly. We need a girl around here to settle these heathens down."

"Sure," she huffs. "*Now* you want a girl. I wanted one three kids ago."

"I told you; I can't have a mini you running around without brothers to look after her. I'm too fucking old to have two of you stressing me out."

"I do not stress you out."

"Baby, all you do is stress me out." I smile, pulling her into a kiss before she can use that smart-ass mouth on me. She melts into me, purring like a little kitten.

A crash sounds from the living room.

I groan, breaking away from her lips. "And that's my cue to get my ass out there before your sons start a riot in the living room."

"They're your sons when they misbehave. They're mine when they're snuggly." She pats me on the chest and then squeezes past me out of the laundry room. "Good luck out there. I'm going to get their stuff ready for baths and bed."

"Traitor."

Her laughter floats back to me.

Author's Note

If you enjoyed Callum's Hope, please consider leaving a review! They mean a lot to me!

Coming next in the Silver Spoon Falls series in Grizz's Passion, which releases in May! Can't wait until then? Make sure you check out Oral Arguments, the latest SSF book, which released on the 10th!

Next from me is The Billionaires' Club Complete Collection (with bonus scenes)! And Dear Mr. Dad Bod, coming in April.

PS: You can grab a copy of Love at First Sight for free this month! The anthology includes 11 steamy instalove romances.

Silver Spoon Falls

Welcome to Silver Spoon Falls, TX. The men here are known for having it all. Except there's a shortage of eligible ladies in town to share it with. These determined men won't let that slow them down. Like the MC brotherhood who calls this small-town home, their best friends, brothers, and neighbors will turn the town on its ear looking for their curvy soulmates in this spin-off series of sweet and steamy instalove romances from Loni Ree, Nichole Rose, and jointly as Loni Nichole.

You've already fallen for the Silver Spoon MC. Now get ready to fall for the single men of Silver Spoon Falls!

Check out the entire Silver Spoon Falls series: mybook.to/SSFalls

Fischer's Catch by Loni Ree - mybook.to/FischersCatchLoniRee

Dillon's Heart by Loni Nichole – mybook.to/DillonsHeart

Adam's Fugitive by Loni Ree - mybook.to/AdamsFugitiveLoniRee

Razor's Flame by Loni Nichole -mybook.to/RazorsFlame

Ryker's Reward by Loni Nichole - mybook.to/RykersReward

Zane's Rebel by Loni Nichole - mybook.to/ZanesRebelLoniNichole

Xavier's Kitten b Nichole Rose - mybook.to/XaviersKitten

Callum's Hope by Nichole Rose - March 14, 2023: mybook.to/CallumsHope

Grizz's Passion by Loni Nichole - May 9th, 2023: mybook.to/GrizzPassion

DEAR MR. DAD BOD

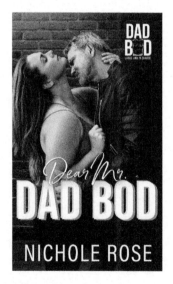

Dear Mr. Dad Bod: Where do I apply to be your baby girl?

Madden Banks

Things I never thought I'd do:

Become social media's resident sexpert, Mr. Dad Bod.

Post thirst traps.

Fall head over heels for a girl half my age.

But here I am, anyway.

The whole world tunes in to ask me burning questions about their kinks and see my dad bod in all its glory.

So it shouldn't be any surprise when they're front and center the day the curvy dancer of my dreams appears.

Olive Crosby has my heart trying to beat out of my chest...and I've never even met her in person.

That's about to change.

This daddy is claiming his little princess, and I don't care who is watching.

Olive Crosby

Being social media's resident curvy dancer can be exhausting.

Everyone knows my name, but no one knows me.

Until the night I slip into Mr. Dad Bod's live stream to ask him the question I've been dying to ask.

Now, everyone knows my secret.

And they know just who I want to fulfill my naughty fantasy.

But I didn't anticipate the whole world tuning in to watch it unfold.

Nor did I expect to fall for the mysterious Madden Banks.

He's everything I expected and so much more.

Can we really make this work, or was asking for a daddy a little too much real for the world to handle?

Watch out! This silver fox and his younger curvy girl are taking your favorite social media app (and heart) by storm in this age-gap romance. If you enjoy OTT possessive older man, instalove goodness, and scorching hot romance, you'll love Madden and Olive's steamy story.

Pre-order live! Coming April 24th!

INSTALOVE BOOK CLUB

The Instalove Book Club is now in session!

Get the inside scoop from your favorite instalove authors, meet new authors to love, and snag freebies and bonus content from featured authors every month. The Instalove Book Club newsletter goes out once per week!

Join now to get your hands on bonus scenes and brand-new, exclusive content from our first six featured authors.

Join the Club: http://instalovebookclub.com

NICHOLE'S BOOK BEAUTIES

Want to connect with Nichole and other readers? We're building a girl gang! Join Nichole Rose's Book Beauties on Facebook for fun, games, and behind-the-scenes exclusives!

Follow Nichole

Sign-up for Nichole's mailing list at http://authorni
cholerose.com/newsletter to stay up to date on all new
releases and for exclusive ARC giveaways from Nichole
Rose.

Want to connect with Nichole and other readers? Join
Nichole Rose's Book Beauties on Facebook!

facebook.com/AuthorNicholeRose/

instagram.com/AuthorNicholeRose

twitter.com/AuthNicholeRose

bookbub.com/authors/nichole-rose

tiktok.com/@authornicholerose

MORE BY NICHOLE ROSE

Her Alpha Series

Her Alpha Daddy Next Door

Her Alpha Boss Undercover

Her Alpha's Secret Baby

Her Alpha Protector

Her Date with an Alpha

Her Alpha: The Complete Series

Her Bride Series

His Future Bride

His Stolen Bride

His Secret Bride

His Curvy Bride

His Captive Bride

His Blushing Bride

His Bride: The Complete Series

Claimed Series

Possessing Liberty

Teaching Rowan

Claiming Caroline

Kissing Kennedy

Claimed: The Complete Series

Love on the Clock Series

Adore You

Hold You

Keep You

Protect You

Love on the Clock: The Complete Series

The Billionaires' Club

The Billionaire's Big Bold Weakness

The Billionaire's Big Bold Wish

The Billionaire's Big Bold Woman

The Billionaire's Big Bold Wonder

Playing for Keeps

Cutie Pie

Ice Breaker

Ice Prince

Ice Giant

The Second Generation

A Blushing Bride for Christmas

Love Bites

Come Undone

Dripping Pearls

Silver Spoon MC

The Surgeon

The Heir

The Lawyer

The Prodigy

The Bodyguard

Silver Spoon MC Collection: Nichole's Crew

Echoes of Forever

His Christmas Miracle

Taken by the Hitman

Wicked Saint

The Ruined Trilogy
Physical Science

Wrecked

Wanton

Destination Romance
Romancing the Cowboy

Beach House Beauty

Standalone Titles
A Touch of Summer

Black Velvet

His Secret Obsession

Dirty Boy

Naughty Little Elf

Tempted by December

Devil's Deceit

A Bride for the Beast (writing with Fern Fraser)

A Hero for Her

Easy on Me
Easy Ride

Easy Surrender

One Night with You
Falling Hard
Model Behavior
Learning Curve
Angel Kisses

Silver Spoon Falls
Xavier's Kitten
Callum's Hope
Snow's Prince
Aurora's Knight (coming soon)

writing with Loni Ree as Loni Nichole
Dillon's Heart
Razor's Flame
Ryker's Reward
Zane's Rebel
Oral Arguments
Grizz's Passion (coming soon)

ABOUT NICHOLE ROSE

Nichole Rose writes filthy, feel-good romance for curvy readers. Her books feature headstrong, sassy women and the alpha males who consume them. From grumpy detectives to country boys with attitude to instalove and over-the-top declarations, nothing is off-limits.

Nichole is sure to have a steamy, sweet story just right for everyone. She fully believes the world is ugly enough without trying to fit falling in love into a one-size-fits-all box.

When not writing, Nichole enjoys fine wine, cute shoes, and everything supernatural. She is happily married to the love of her life and is a proud mama to the world's most ridiculous fur-babies. She and her husband live in the Pacific Northwest.

You can learn more about Nichole and her books at authornicholerose.com.

facebook.com/AuthorNicholeRose/

instagram.com/AuthorNicholeRose

twitter.com/AuthNicholeRose

bookbub.com/authors/nichole-rose

tiktok.com/@authornicholerose

Printed in Great Britain
by Amazon